Kneel Down

CHELLE BLISS
EDEN BUTLER

NAVY

Kneel Down

Publisher © Chelle Bliss & Eden Butler
April 23rd 2019
Editor: Silently Judging Your Grammar
Proofreader: Julie Deaton
Cover Design: Lori Jackson
Paperback Formatting: Allusion Graphics, LLC

Prologue
Gin

L ove doesn't come easy when you aren't real sure what it's supposed to look like.

It didn't look familiar at any time in my life. That happens when you've been set aside and tossed away by the people who made you.

But sometimes, the family you're landed with isn't the family of your heart. They aren't who holds you up. They aren't who has your back and makes sure nothing or no one keeps you down.

My family came to me in a dirty redneck bar on the outskirts of Seattle.

It was the first time I laid eyes on Dale Hunter.

Just happened to be in the middle of a bar fight.

He wasn't helping. Wasn't his fight. But he stood there, watching me. A grin moving the right corner of his mouth like he couldn't believe a long-legged thing like me knew how to handle loud rednecks who had no upbringing and lousy manners.

That grin almost distracted me when I jumped on the asshole's back, waving a hand in Dale's direction as he watched.

"Hand that over," I told him, pointing to a bottle just behind him on a speaker.

Bastard kept right on grinning like somehow he knew I didn't need his help. Like he knew just by getting a good look at me that I'd manage fine on my own.

"Well?"

"Half full. Seems a shame to waste," he said.

Had to give him that one. So, I did what any East Tennessee woman worth her salt would do—I downed it, then knocked that redneck out with it when it was empty.

Dale bought me a drink and decided right then I'd be his friend no matter if I wanted to or not.

I did.

I kept on being his friend. Even when his obnoxious wife, Trudy, announced to our work crew that her man was off-limits, though everyone knew that already. Even when he refused to see what everyone else did— that Trudy was loose and easy.

Through all that, I stuck by him because he was my friend. But on that first night, in the middle of a bar fight, that smooth bastard half grinned at me, looking impressed and amused all at the same time, and something that shouldn't have clicked inside my head: Dale Hunter was for me.

God help me.

It was the "for me" part that was messing up my thought process. Especially when that wife of his finally showed Dale her true colors and ran off, breaking his heart in the process.

Years had passed between that bar fight and now. Somehow, I was still picking up the pieces.

We were supposed to be on watch. There was a stalker approaching, and it was our job to make sure that asshole steered cleared of the cabin and our friend Kiel's wife, Cara, inside. Seems the man her father wanted her to marry didn't take kindly to her announcement that she'd been married years back to a man her daddy had never approved of.

Now, we were on alert.

Or, I was.

With my best friend Dale, drinking coffee laced with whiskey. He smelled delicious, looked beautiful, and sat just inches from me.

Damn it.

"You want some more coffee?" he asked, nudging the thermos at me. I nodded, pulling the thick coat tighter around my waist as I leaned forward. The flame on the fire pit was getting low, and I stoked a half-burned log. Dale took my mug and refilled it. "Whiskey?"

"Yeah."

"If they come from the south, we're screwed..." he started, yet another SEAL monologue about perimeter security and impending threats and the best way to go about eliminating them.

Dale wasn't boring. We'd spent hours at a time with no lulls in our conversations, talking about everything and anything. But when he got specific about defense strategy or strategic measures of security, he lost me.

Like now.

I hid a yawn behind my mug, but he caught it.

Pausing mid-explanation of something to do with minimizing damage to civilians, he looked down at me. "You unable to hang?"

"Check yourself." I ruffled the thick jacket on his shoulder, twisting the hoodie to the side to make a pillow for myself. "Civilian here." He didn't complain when I leaned against him, holding my mug under my chin. The coffee was still warm, and the heat helped to cut the biting temperatures that seemed to be turning my lips blue. "You keep talking about defense measures against some mafia stalker, and I'll be snoring in under a minute."

"Fair enough," Dale said, leaning back against his chair. He took me with him, resting a hand over my temple to adjust my position on his shoulder. "If I talk about other things, will you stay awake?"

"Why?" I glanced up at him, grinning when I caught his gaze. There was nothing I liked more in the world than messing with Dale Hunter, except maybe the way his eyes looked when I did it. They went glassy and bright, like just me teasing him made something light up inside him. "You feeling all lonesome and scared out here? Want me to stay up and keep you company?"

"Yeah," he deadpanned. "I managed four tours in Fallujah—two in places I'm not at liberty to discuss—but I need a knock-kneed redhead to protect me from some asshole with a bruised ego."

"Shut up," I said, punching his arm. "You love my knock-knees." I snuggled closer, the day's activity catching up with me, not thinking too much about the idea that Dale didn't disagree with me. "And my red hair."

He took a minute and went so quiet I'd almost dozed off before he moved. I felt the slow swipe of his callused thumbs moving over my forehead. "Can't say I don't, Gingerbread."

He'd used that nickname for me a thousand times. Not too clever, if I was being honest. My name, my red hair, Dale's favorite cookie, and I got saddled with the nickname. But there was something different in the way he said it then, voice all soft, a little sweeter than I'd ever heard it before.

Could be I was hearing things I wanted.

Could be the whiskey getting to me.

But I still held my breath, not quite sure what he meant or why Dale had said that, *how* he'd said that.

We'd been skirting around whatever had been between us for a long time. We were friends. Nothing more for a very long time. Trudy was his wife, and I'd never disrespected that, no matter what that insane woman accused me of.

Then she wasn't anyone's wife anymore.

Then I was just his friend who'd pick him up when he was too drunk to drive after drowning his misery over his cheating wife with bourbon and blondes.

Then...one day, one normal, ordinary day of us fetching each other coffee, of us asking what we'd do for lunch, of us planning what we'd get up to that weekend, of him taking me to the doctor when my Chevy was in the shop, of me hauling his butt in for his yearly checkups at the VA when he refused to go on his own, of that night at Lucky's when Otis Redding started singing about loving his woman too long and Dale grabbed me, held me close for a slow, buzzed but sensual dance, I'd realized we weren't just friends anymore. He'd held me too tight that night.

Like he wanted me.

Like he knew how much I wanted him.

Like he didn't care who saw all that wanting spanning the half-inch space between us as we danced. Whatever moved between us felt like a pulse, a heartbeat that kept me living, but I'd never been too sure if he felt it too.

Just then, with my head on Dale's shoulder, with his voice soft and low and that pet name coming out of his mouth like a wish, I thought maybe he had.

My breath stilled in my lungs. I felt Dale shift, a movement that didn't adjust me from his shoulder or disturb any sleep he thought I was getting.

"I'd do anything for you," he whispered, like he was sure I couldn't hear him. "I'd never let anyone touch you. Not some mafia asshole. Not anyone." Then, his voice lower, his words fierce, Dale said something that made the breath catch in my throat. "I'd die to protect you."

I couldn't move, too scared I'd spook him. Petrified he'd take it all back.

Dale came closer. The heat from his body killing the chill that had set upon my skin as the fire grew lower and lower. I caught the faint whiff of his hair, something that reminded me of his normal scent, sweat and the rosewood soap his little sister made for him back in New Orleans. Then the warm, sweet sensation of his breath fanning across my face as he lowered. He didn't touch me. Didn't move my chin up to set me in position. Dale didn't thread his fingers through my hair or do anything at all that told me he had to have me or wanted to devour my lips. He simply bent closer, moved slowly, and brought his full, wide mouth to mine.

One long, slow brush of his salty-sweet kiss against my criminally unused mouth, my mind counting the seconds until breath became necessary, then Dale leaned back.

He moved his gaze over my face, but his focus was on my mouth. He stared at my lips for a long time like he wanted another taste. Just as suddenly as the kiss had come, he moved his eyebrows up, surprise transforming his hungry features as though he hadn't expected I'd been awake for that sweet, simple kiss.

I couldn't help myself.

He'd taken.

He'd tasted.

I wanted my turn.

The look he gave me came from somewhere Dale had never shown me before. There was heat, want, and a lot of passion tied up in that look. I'd seen something similar to it in the mirror anytime I found myself zoning out to thoughts of him while I washed my face or fixed myself up before we went out.

He began to move away completely, but I caught him. I touched his face to keep him close, stealing the kiss I'd always craved. It lasted longer this time. He let me control it. Let me slip my fingertips into his hair. He didn't whine or complain when I put a little pressure on his mouth, but when I let the smallest slip of my tongue touch his bottom lip, Dale released a low, guttural moan deep in his throat and broke away from me. His breath came out slow from his mouth, control slipping as he looked down at me.

A million questions shifted in his eyes.

A million more scattered around my head, but we went on staring at each other. Not speaking. Not moving, both seeming a little out of control. A little lost until Dale wet his lips and watched me a half a second longer before a shudder took hold of me, quaking up my spine, making that hungry look on his face vanish.

"You cold?"

"Something like that," I told him, not brave enough to let him know the temperature outside had no effect on my body and the chill that had taken over it.

"Come on. Let's get inside." He stood, grabbing hold of my hand to lead me off the balcony. "We can watch good enough through the glass doors."

I followed him into the blistering warmth of the Kaino cabin, the awkward tension thickening the air between us. The house was silent except for the low moans coming from upstairs belonging to Kiel and his wife, Cara. They were living their lives, taking advantage of the calm before any danger came. Because it *was* coming. It was likely on its way right now. Kiel and Cara loved each other. Why wouldn't they spend whatever moments there were left in the thick of that love?

Dale moved two chairs in front of the glass doors, but neither of us sat. The moaning grew louder. I closed my eyes, aware of him behind me, of the stinging of my lips where he'd just been, of Kiel and Cara and the sounds they made. I moved closer to the door, watching, anxious, forgetting that the man behind me was the person I loved most in the world.

The kiss shouldn't have changed us so quickly. But it had, and the shift between us now teetered between good and bad, between want and need. We didn't speak or comment on anything at all. Dale stood just behind me, watching the woods surrounding the cabin and the stillness of the early morning around us.

We kissed, I told myself. Those two words getting no less shocking no matter how often I repeated them to myself.

We kissed. Just now.

How many times had I dreamed about him kissing me? How many hours had I spent like a damn teenager watching him talk, memorizing the exact shape of his mouth and every line in his perfectly arched lips? God, I was ridiculous. It couldn't be helped. Dale Hunter had always been a force of nature, and with one kiss, he'd consumed me.

I'd been taken over by Typhoon Hunter.

There was only the crackle of the flame in the fireplace and the slow click of the grandfather clock in the den to break the silence. Above us, Kiel and Cara quieted, though I could still make out the low, constant thump of something hitting the wall. I couldn't stand it for a second longer.

"Maybe we should walk the perimeter." I cleared my throat, wondering if I sounded as stupid to him as I did to myself. "Like you mentioned earlier." I inclined my head, looking out the glass door when two doe moved through a grouping of trees at the back of the property. "You...want to do that?"

He didn't answer.

I glanced up, frowning when I couldn't make out his reflection in the glass above my head. Somehow, I knew what would happen if I turned to face him. The room was too still. He was too silent, and the moment had not passed. If I turned to face him, everything would change.

We would change.

I had to trust it would be for the best.

Inhaling, I pressed my lips together, glancing over my shoulder to catch his expression before I turned my body to face him, chin lifted, expression expectant. "Dale?"

He didn't want to scan the perimeter. That much I could tell from how tightly he worked his jaw. Dale moved his head once, his gaze lowering over my face, down my body, then up again before he took his step. The look he gave me was a small warning I wasn't sure was for me or himself. "I...got other...things..."

I tilted my head, not expecting the explanation. Not understanding what sense it was supposed to make. "What...other things?"

"Things..." he said, taking two more steps. He didn't smile. Dale didn't do anything but look down at me. His expression serious. Determined. "Things I want from you."

"Things..." I swallowed. My back hit the glass door when he moved closer. "What...things?"

"These fucking things."

It took two seconds for Dale to make up his mind. At least, that's how long it seemed to me. He moved closer still, hand outstretched, palm flat against the glass above my head. With his free hand, Dale shifted his touch to my chin, cupping it to move my mouth closer to his. He didn't rush. He didn't come to me in a panicked, desperate frenzy. There was a heat in his eyes that warned of the storm brewing behind his practiced control.

"Dale..."

"You kissed me back," he said simply, as though it explained what had changed his attitude. Touch moving down my neck, he nudged so close that I had to stand flat against the door. It still wasn't close enough for me. When he spoke, some of Dale's control frayed loose. "Never thought you'd kiss me back, Gingerbread."

"Always wanted to."

He moved back, eyebrows shifting up as though he couldn't believe me.

He relaxed when I grabbed his face, loving how his skin felt against my palm. "Always," I promised.

He took exactly one-point-three seconds to look at me, eyelashes still, black eyes glistening, full, sweet lips parted as he stared—a frozen picture of every fantasy I'd ever had standing right in front of me.

And then Dale Hunter, my best friend, lost control.

As he lowered his mouth to mine, Dale gripped my leg, giving me his tongue while he drew my thigh against him.

"You taste like..."

"Who cares?" I said, needing him quiet. If he talked, I couldn't feel his tongue against mine. I'd miss that salty-sweet taste of him invading my senses. "Just...don't stop kissing me..."

He was a SEAL. He took direction like a trooper.

Dale gripped my leg high as I wrapped my arms around his neck and found the hem of his shirt beneath the thick fabric of his coat and encountered warm, smooth skin. It seemed every touch I gave him set him off. Did something to him that no one had done before.

He made low, deep sounds that vibrated against my neck as he kissed me. Just the sound had my heart ramming hard. Had my insides whirling. "Dale..." The name came out in a whimper when he nibbled at my neck, then a sharper moan when he sucked my skin into his mouth. *"Fuck."*

The sound of that filthy word coming out of my mouth seemed to do something to him. I felt the length of him as he pushed my shoulders against the glass door and took my other leg in his hand to wrap my legs around his waist.

He paused. He looked up with his features tight and eyes sharp. "Should we..."

I silenced that good sense by attacking his neck, loving the tangy taste of his skin against my tongue. Dale grunted, resting one hand on the glass as he held me up with his free hand. He was strong everywhere. Hard *everywhere*. I was overcome by all the sensation he worked inside me. All that strength. All that power, crying out when I kissed him, when I teased his nipples with my nails and pushed my pussy against him.

"Dale...*please*..." I cried, knowing what I was asking for was too much, too fast, too ridiculous. But I was lost in a fog of lust and want.

I'd waited too long for this.

I didn't want to wait anymore.

"Gin..." He breathed against my chest. His fingers curled in my shirt as he pushed off me. He didn't put more than a few inches between us and still kept his mouth near mine. His breath warming over my skin with each exhale. "I...I don't know what we're doing here..." I opened my mouth, ready to beg him not to stop if the thought came to him, but Dale shook his head, lowering to his knees in front of me. "Don't much care about right and wrong right now." He pushed me back, his wide, strong hands cupping my ass as he looked up at me. That single glance made me wet. Made me hold my breath waiting for his next move, the next second when any indecision left him. "All I know is I need to taste you." He watched me as he moved one hand to my stomach, pushing up my shirt and placing a slow, wet kiss over my navel. "I need to taste you everywhere, Gingerbread."

Fuck's sake. I could have melted on the spot.

I could only watch him when he slid that thick, hot tongue along my stomach. His attention still on me, my nipple hardening, my insides liquefying as he teased me. Dale knew how to seduce. He knew what one look, one slow, smooth glance could do to a woman who wanted him, and right then, I'd never wanted anyone more.

He slipped his eyes closed when I moved my fingers in his hair. I gave him no resistance to the tug he made on my jeans as he lowered them over my hips, his full, thick lips caressing each hipbone, sliding over the sensible cotton boyshorts I wore as he pulled those down too.

"Look at you," he said, the words coming out in a gravel of sound that made Dale sound drunk. "Fucking hell, baby, look at you…" He didn't wait. He stopped teasing me completely, and Dale lowered. His gaze on my pussy, grunting as he leaned closer to lick me there. "So fucking tempting. So beautiful."

I could barely stand from the motion of his mouth against me and the increasing rhythm of my heart thundering like I was midway through a marathon. When Dale slipped two fingers inside me and I arched, meeting his mouth, pulling him closer with my hand to the back of his head, he took over completely.

In one quick sweep, he broke away from me, picking me up to pull me against his waist. His fingers tangled in my hair as he walked us in front of the fire and laid me to the floor.

"Fucking perfect, Gingerbread…better than I ever thought…" He silenced himself. That long, wide body strong, imposing as he kissed me again. He slipped down my body, cupping my ass again. He pushed my center to his mouth to tease me again and again until I couldn't see anything but the stars that shot behind my eyes as my orgasm crested.

"Dale..." My voice throbbed. My heart slowed, but I still reached for him, needing him close. Still amazed that I had him here, with me, in a blaze of activity and heat and lust and impossible potential. None of this seemed real, but there he was, moving closer. Moving over me with the background of the forest in the glass doors behind us and the fire at our side.

"Gin..."

I held my hand over his mouth, scared what he'd say. I was terrified he'd give me some explanation my heart couldn't bear to hear, but Dale didn't try to make excuses. He kissed my fingers, pushing my hand aside before he moved up my body.

There seemed to be so much he wanted to say. I saw it all moving across his features, shifting the hard lines between his eyebrows and tightening the muscles in his neck. But Dale didn't speak. He just moved closer, holding my face in his hand. He kissed me like he couldn't get enough of the way I tasted.

It was heaven. A living daydream made real. I never wanted it to end. I wished nothing would stop this moment. I meant to pull him close. He was ready, I could feel as much in the hard outline of his cock against my leg and in the greedy way he touched me, like he was losing control and didn't care that he was. I reached for him, ready to tell him I wanted him right then, just like that, raw and real right in front of that fire, to have him inside me, to feel him everywhere. He moaned, loud, a little desperate when I lowered his zipper. His thick bottom lip denting behind his teeth as he waited for me to release him. But when I moved my attention from that zipper and the warmth I cupped between my fingers, to the movement just over Dale's shoulders, I froze. Two men moved around on the other side of the door, both with guns, running across the balcony. "Dale..."

He glanced at my face, spotting the twist I made with my chin. He jerked his attention to the glass door behind us. We were shadowed by the darkness in the cabin. Dale slipped off me, crouching as he adjusted his clothes. I hurried to pull up my jeans and lower my shirt. We crawled away from the exposure of the glass doors, to the back of the room near the stairs. We watched from the edge of the room as two large men with guns drawn looked around the doorframe—one fiddling with the lock, the other glancing inside.

Dale moved his lips against my ear. "Stay quiet and low to the floor." Dale withdrew the Glock from the holster at his ankle and took off the safety. "I'll lock the door. You stay out of the way. Get to Kane or Kiel if you can, but only if it's safe."

I opened my mouth, ready to argue, but he shook his head, silencing me.

"Please don't argue with me, Gin. This is what I do." He leaned closer, attention on the porch, lips on my cheek. "You know I don't say it because...the words... they don't mean much. But...in case the chance gets away from me, you gotta know, Gingerbread..." He paused, throat working like something had gotten stuck there. "I...you're the only one who matters to me." And then Dale disappeared through the glass doors and landed in the middle of chaos.

Dale

"Where is she?" I asked as I stepped into the cabin, happy to be alive and pick up where Gin and I had left off before my ass took a bullet. I waved off the bodyguards behind me, all of them leftovers from the mafia bullshit the Carelli family brought to this cabin. Kane stood, taking my quick slap to his shoulder as he and Kiel greeted me.

"Out there," Kiel said, motioning with his head toward the balcony.

"Tread lightly," Kane told me as I took a step toward Gin where she sat outside with Cara and Kit in front of the fire pit. Hell, she looked beautiful, and I stood there watching her, my head shaking as Kane went on telling me how my fuckup had messed with her. "She's not in a good way."

"Pfft," Kiel muttered, saying something I couldn't quite understand.

The doctors at the hospital had me so hopped up on pain meds, I didn't remember a damn thing from the last few days. I'd finally put my foot down and refused any more medicine because I needed to get myself straight to face Gin after the shit Kane told me I'd said in front of her. I caught Kit's attention first when she stood with Gin's empty glass in her hand, appreciating the smile she gave me. It gave me a small boost of encouragement, but it wouldn't be enough to clue me in on exactly how Gin felt. Kit gripped my hand as she passed me but didn't speak, and I moved to the door, inhaling as I glanced at Cara before I pulled it open.

I tried to keep my expression calm. Tried like hell not to rush out there and get Gin to face me, but the look on her face stopped me cold. I felt Cara watching me as I looked down at Gin, knew the woman was likely judging me. But my attention was on that beautiful redhead and her full mouth, the smooth skin and those sweet features that I'd made go all tight and hard with the bullshit I'd caused.

Gin didn't turn around as I stepped onto the wooden balcony. She sat still in the chair, body curled and rigid, and when I spoke one word, managing a low, soft "Gingerbread," my best friend jerked her gaze right at me. She stood, pushing the chair behind her, and I readied myself for the shitstorm I knew I had coming.

She leveled one long look my way, glaring down at my hand when I offered it to her.

"Say...something," I tried, trying to reach for her and getting nothing but her hard stare. When Gin's mouth tightened even further, I shot for laughter. "Reckon you can call me pincushion. Got another hole punch..." I motioned to my gut, even forced out a loud laugh, but I still got zero response.

The air around us blew against her hair, and I picked up the scent of wine from her breath when she exhaled. Something deep inside me wanted to get drunk on her, wanted to taste her, just a little, but Gin curled her arms over her chest, the movement like a shield to keep me away as she shook her head, grabbing the door before she took off into the cabin.

She didn't want an audience. I knew that. Stepping into the house, grabbing a beer from Kane when he offered it, I knew that. But I could wait. She'd expect me to. That was how we'd played this thing between us.

We'd wait until the time was right.

Three a.m. was the witching hour. Gin never slept then, something she'd clued me in on the first time I'd recovered from a bender on her sofa and woke up to find her out on her front porch drinking coffee.

"Foster asshole number six used to come in at three a.m., drunk, mad at the world, and looking for a punching bag. We'd have to see who was smartest, fastest, and quiet enough to avoid his fists," she'd explained like it was a fact that she recalled, not a bad memory that kept her up at night.

"You always won?" I'd asked her, still drunk.
"Still here, ain't I?"

At 3:05, I found Gin in the living room, sock-footed, with her ankles crossed as she sat in front of the roaring fireplace. Her eyes were unfocused as she watched the flames, and I moved behind her, exhaling only when she didn't flinch as I slid an arm around her waist to hold her. "I've missed you," I whispered in her ear as I inhaled the sweetness of her red hair.

When there was no response, I brushed the hair away from her neck and pressed my lips to the soft spot just below her ear. She shivered through a long sigh.

"Ginger—"

"Stop," she said, cutting me off.

Anger pulsed from her, and something sharp splintered in my gut. This would take more than an apology. Seemed that kiss I remembered giving her had done more damage than I thought. But what else had I'd done? Run my mouth about my stupid ex in the hospital, yeah, but she had to know that was the medicine talking. Gin knew me. She knew what she meant to me even if I hadn't found the balls to admit how I felt. This reaction? Her anger? It should have dimmed by now.

"Do you know how badly you hurt me?"

I ran my fingertip over the curve of her shoulder. "I didn't mean to scare you."

I knew my getting shot would set us back some. Watching fellow soldiers take a bullet had done something to me; I couldn't imagine how it would've felt if it had been Gin instead of me. That would've been a heartache and a guilt I never would've overcome.

"Scare me?" she whispered, but not in that sweet, gentle way either. "Are you shitting me right now?"

I tightened my arms around her waist, because we were going to hash this shit out and move on with our lives. Get back to the sweet spot we were heading toward. That kiss was the first step. I wanted more. A hell of a lot more. "Well, yeah. I mean, I know how it feels to watch someone take a bullet. I think we..."

She wiggled out of my arms and spun to face me. "Do you love me?" she asked.

"I..." *Damn it.* I hadn't whispered those words to another soul since Trudy ripped my heart into a million pieces with her cheating ways. "I..." I repeated with the words hanging on the tip of my tongue. But no matter how hard I tried, I couldn't make them come.

"Dale, I thought we were going somewhere. Becoming something bigger. That night," she said, her eyes glassy with tears, "before all hell broke loose, and you...we... When all that *happened*..." I frowned, wondering why she'd gone all shy on me about a little bit of kissing. She paused, swallowing hard before she shook her head. "For a moment, I thought I felt something bigger than friendship and lust."

"You did." I reached for her, but she moved too quickly for me to catch her with the number of fucking stitches lining my torso.

"Standing here." She stepped forward and touched my face so softly I thought she was about to forgive me.

I'd always been able to read people, especially Gin. She was my best friend, helping me through more shit than I wanted to remember. She'd seen me at my worst and my very best, never judging me because that was how we were with each other.

She moved her mouth close to mine, and I could feel her warm, sweet breath as it rolled over my lips. "I can easily say I love you. But you can't seem to find the words."

"Gin, you know I'm not good with any of that."

She shook her head, and her soft eyes narrowed, growing icy. She dropped her hand to her side, and her warmth vanished. "You had no problem saying it to Trudy. In fact, you said a lot of shit to Trudy right in front of me."

"I didn't mean any of that, Gin. You know that."

She stood, curling her arms to her chest again, putting as much space between us as she could. "You didn't mean them then, but they rolled right off your tongue. Now, I'm here, asking you to tell me how you feel about me, and I get you're 'not good with any of that'?"

"I was so drugged up, Gin. I didn't know what I was saying."

"I get that medicine doesn't make you right in the head, Dale, but you could've said those words to me

anytime. Hell, you could say them to me right now."
She crossed her arms, and I knew that look in her eyes.

I was fucked.

Battles were my game. I fought because it was in my nature not to let shit stand, not shit that broke people. Not shit that was unfair or unjust or on the bad side of brutal. My job as a SEAL had made me hard. It had demanded that I set aside thought, consideration, and just get the mission completed. Me and battle, we got tight. We stayed tight through Fallujah and Afghanistan. We got damn indistinguishable during the Congo extraction.

They'd all been battles I'd fought, ones that leveled me so low, I thought I might never recover from the fall I took.

Guns and glory came easily to me.

Emotions, entanglements, and mustering the nerve to say I'm sorry? Not so much.

But this right here? This was a clusterfuck I was sure I wouldn't survive.

"It was the medicine...honest, Gingerbread."

"No," Gin said, crossing her arms tight against her, like she needed to keep herself back from me, like there was some sort of danger in standing three feet away from me. "You don't get to call me that. Not anymore."

I felt like an asshole for the shit I couldn't say. For the shit I wanted to say every second of my life.

Her face got redder, her temper surfacing, and I held my breath, angling a look over her face, hazarding the level of pissed off she was. Could have been "Might not wanna talk to me," but was most likely "Motherfucker, I'm gonna cut you." I wasn't a stupid man. I damn well knew to keep my paces, measure the mood when a woman was itching to snip your balls.

"I...don't get to call you the same nickname I've used for two years now?"

"No. You dang sure don't." The eastern Tennessee twang surfaced, a sure sign Gin was twisting a few loud curses and her lethal temper below the surface of all that smooth, pale skin.

"Because I got friendly with my ex?" She didn't answer but gave her lips a twitching snarl. Close enough to a "yeah," for me. "Because I got...friendly with my ex while I was hopped up on morphine..." Another snarl, but this time, the twitching quickened. Had to be careful here. "Because I got...friendly with my ex while I was hopped up on morphine...after getting shot by some mafia roughneck?"

Jaw working into a tight clench, Gin looked out over the balcony, going rigid when I took a step closer to her. She was probably the best friend I had. Used to be able to say that about my kid brother, Anthony, even about our baby sister, Jazmine, but everything went to hell when Tony got messed up with some dealers back home in New Orleans. We all went to pieces when we lost our mother.

Shit went sideways with Gin a year back. One too many times of her picking my ass up off my floor. One too many mornings of me waking up from a drunken stupor with my head in her lap and her fingers scrubbing away the pounding ache in my head. She was good to me when I was nothing but trouble for her. She mattered to me. She mattered a lot, but I'd figured out when people mattered to you, they got hurt. Couldn't have her hurt. Not ever.

"Gin, please let me just..." Words weren't my thing, never had been, but there was some desperate, irritating throb down in my gut that wanted me to spew out fucking poetry if it meant she'd forgive me. I was a SEAL. I didn't do the sweet-talk bullshit. When it came to women, I'd relied on the way I looked, counting on the rugged roughneck thing I had going to get me some company.

But I wasn't looking to fuck Gin. I was looking to get her forgiveness. I just wished to God I could remember everything I'd done to warrant me needing to ask for it. A bullet to the gut and a three-hour surgery sort of messed me around. That shit made my head fuzzy, and I had no real memory of what happened. There'd been a fight, a bloody one from what Kane told me, then bullets flying, then me hopped up on morphine. But hell if I could remember anything from the day I left set the Friday before until the morning after my surgery. Short-term memory loss they called it. Something to do with a bad reaction to the anesthesia. Go figure.

"There isn't anything to say." She sounded tired, like the shitshow that had been our lives for weeks now was one she just couldn't handle anymore. She seemed to like her anger. Seemed like it kept her company better than I ever had. "Doesn't matter, does it? You saying that shit. You saying that shit to *her*. She *was* your wife." She looked at me then, her face twisted into tight lines and hard points. "When it comes down to it, Trudy is the one you married. That doesn't die easy."

"It does when she did her best to kill it every day." I got closer, holding up my hands when she jerked back. I held my breath, hoping my attempt at surrender kept her calm enough not to bolt on me. Gin did that when she'd crossed the "Motherfucker, I'm gonna cut you" level and hopped right into the "You are dead to me" zone. Breathing helped. At least, it helped settle the tension between us before I continued. "You know better than to think I'd still want her, that I want anyone but..."

She waited. Took her turn at controlled breathing. I saw the question as it worked between her eyes. Gin needed me to admit the thing... I just couldn't. She wanted me to say the words I hadn't been able to utter to a soul since my cheating ex-wife had ripped them from my heart.

"You know..." I rubbed my neck, hating that everything I wanted to say got clogged in my chest, like something pushed it further and further into my stomach the longer I stood there searching for words I couldn't make come out of my mouth. "I'm...sorry, Gin. I just..."

The words died right there, somewhere between the frozen stare she gave me and the breath she held as she waited for me to finish speaking. But I couldn't. Nothing would come. Things got twisted inside me when I thought about her in any way that wasn't friendly. I squashed what I wanted because I knew anything else would end badly. It always did.

Just then, I wanted her to reach inside me and extract the words. I needed a little help, but I knew she'd probably gotten sick of helping me figure out how to navigate my fucked-up life. Just then, I think my best friend gave up on me.

Gin shook her head, temper firing back up until her cheeks were nearly the same color red as all that wild, ginger hair that circled her head like a mane.

"You can take your apologies and shove them right up your narrow behind!"

The woman wasn't kidding. Cheeks brightening, I knew Gin meant business.

She was off the balcony and down the hall before I could catch the door. I angled around it and went after her, waving off Kane and the others. I needed her to hear me out. I needed Gin to understand why I couldn't say the only thing that mattered to her.

But I came to her room just as she slammed the door, the wood vibrating in the frame, slapping against my nose. That was proof enough of the business my Gingerbread meant.

I'd wait her out. She'd come around. She had to. No one knew me better than Gin. She knew the fucked-up shit I went through with Trudy and how saying those words wasn't as easy as it once was.

Chapter One
Dale

Present day - Seattle

Kane was the storm. At least, he had been. But then the storm Kane had been petered out any time Kit got too near him.

She was the storm chaser and had caught him completely.

Looking at him now, that stupid smile stretching over his mug, I figured the storm would only show itself when she wasn't around or when Kane wasn't in the middle of celebrating his pending ball and chain... Scratch that.

Kit wasn't like Trudy.

Let's see... The phrase, I supposed, would be *pending nuptials.*

Despite it being my third glass, the whiskey in my hand burned all the way down when I drank deep. I avoided Kit and the makeup women who swarmed around her, ogling her ring and the flowers for the wedding she and Kane would host in a few days.

I never liked crowds much. Liked wearing a sports jacket even less, but there I stood, shoulder against a column that separated the back of the bar from the dance floor, sipping on my whiskey and hiding like an asshole because I didn't want to be here.

"It's a few hours out of your life," Kane had promised the night he'd hemmed and hawed before he sacked up enough to ask me to stand up for him at his wedding. Didn't get the big job. That would be on Kiel, Kane's brother, thank Christ. But I still had to stand up at that altar, looking like an asshole while Kane and Kit grinned and carried on like idiots as some preacher made them promise their "I dos" would be "I always dos."

The looking like a schmuck in my jacket was one thing. Standing up there trying not to grumble too much was another. But the damn trot back down the aisle...with Gin on my arm...was something altogether different.

"Not gonna happen," I'd told Kit when she'd gone all sweet eyes and dimpled smiles on me a few weeks back on set. She'd just laid down the hammer—told me who she'd paired me up with for the monkey show of a wedding.

"Please, Dale?" Another eye blink, and the woman went on with her explanation. "Gin's been so busy with the new set in Portland, so she couldn't be my maid of honor. Since Cara and Kiel are living here again and Cara's all pregnant and idle, well, she agreed to do it for me. It's just a matter of convenience, and you and Gin..."

The glare I shot her way at least kept Kit from blinking those doe eyes at me again.

"Well. It would mean an awful lot to Kane and me if you could play nice and just walk Gin up and down the aisle. Two times, that's it." She'd tilted her head, and the sweet smile I figured had caught Kane's attention years back started to work on me. "You *were* friends, and we're all supposed to be real live grown-ups here, aren't we?"

Kit didn't laugh outright when I grunted, holding back a comment about how un-adult-like it was to let your best friend walk right out of your life when you couldn't muster the stones to ask her to stay. One widening grin over Kit's pretty face and I got why Kane was so sprung over her.

"Shit," I'd said, head shaking when Kit let loose a sound I'd heard only come from females before. "I can be an adult."

"I bet you can!" Whether Kit believed me, I never found out. One non-answer that she took for a yes and the woman skipped away from me, heading straight for Kane across the set.

I'd agreed to the stand-in, but that didn't mean I was anywhere close to being ready to see Gin again.

Hell, for a SEAL I was acting like a chickenshit.

Tonight would be some sort of reception for the incoming wedding party. Then there was a big rehearsal dinner tomorrow. It was a fucking miracle the way Kit wrangled everyone, but even the thunder of activity surrounding me and the swirl of laughter and music filling the small bar as we waited for whatever we were supposed to be waiting for did nothing to distract me.

Not when the door opened and Gin stood there, the light behind her pumping through the dark club, curving around her like a spotlight, making her look like she glowed.

Holy fucking hell.

That couldn't be her.

That wasn't my flannel-shirt-and-Levi's-wearing friend. It wasn't the woman who'd get filthy with me running trails up Mount Rainier or tearing down old barns for scrap when the opportunity came our way. My Gin slung back beers at Lucky's on dollar night and ate burgers and fries with her elbows on the table and her hair pulled back in a sloppy, all over the place bun.

The Gin I'd been missing for a year was absolutely beautiful, something I'd have to be blind and ignorant not to notice no matter what she wore, but *hell*. I'd never seen her looking like she did now. The woman standing in the doorway was someone else entirely— all curves and wildness, hair like a damn sunset in the middle of autumn, a riot of golds and auburn, complementing her pale, perfect skin.

Did my best not to watch her too closely.

Failed miserably.

She walked through the door wearing a dress. A damn, honest-to-God, not-at-all-jeans dress. Never seen that before on Gin. Couldn't say I hated it in the least.

It was black, fit her like a second skin at the top, cut a little low, but flared out around her curvy hips. My mouth watered just looking at her. I downed what was left of my whiskey to keep the hunger I felt working up in me at bay.

"Hey, man, can you help me with the chairs in the back?" Kiel asked, nudging me when I went on watching Gin as she walked through the door and made a beeline for Kit. "Dale?" he asked, punching my shoulder when I ignored him.

"Yeah," I finally said, dropping off my empty glass on the counter of the bar where I stood.

"What are you..." Kiel stopped, the humor lifting in his tone as he turned to stare across the room.

Gin stood between Kit and Kiel's wife, Cara.

"Damn," he said. "She cleans up well."

I answered with a grunt, figuring anything I said, Kiel would use to twist into an insult. I followed the asshole to the back of the bar, nodding to a few of the bartenders and waitstaff as they moved stacks of chairs into the room.

"No response?" Kiel asked, picking up one of the chairs among the stack lining the brick wall at the back of the bar. I didn't much care for his stupid smirk or the way he looked at my face like he expected me to yell at him. "See, Dale, that's what I like about you." I gave him nothing as he went on, a stupid laugh making his voice lift an octave. "No bullshit professions. No real insults except for the constant scowl that twists up your ugly mug." His smile widened when I grabbed a chair and unfolded it with too much force before I moved it next to the one Kiel had just placed at an empty table. "No, no, seriously," he went on, ignoring the glare I gave him. "You go all stoic and silent. Not many people do that when they're irritated, and I gotta say, man, you always seem to be irritated."

"You 'bout done?"

"Fucking with you?" He stopped, holding a chair in his hands when I grabbed another one from the stack. "Fuck no."

I shoved a metal chair under the table before I walked away, leaving Kiel to handle his shit on his own.

"Come on, man, I was just..."

"Lay off," Kane said, waving his kid brother back as he walked into the room.

He followed me to stand in front of the windows that ran the length of the back. Good view out this way, showing off Seattle around us and in the distance, the stretch of Mount Rainier.

It was those peaks I focused on as Kane stood next to me, offering me a refill of my whiskey. "Figured you were sticking to Jack since we're here for the week and don't have to drive back to the set."

I gave him a nod of thanks, then grabbed the glass. I ignored the laughter coming from Kiel as he and a skeleton crew of waitstaff finished unfolding the chairs. We both turned, glancing at Kiel behind us before the activity outside those windows caught our attention again.

"It'd be better if we were back on set."

"It can wait." Kane took a sip from his beer, his attention on the cityscape. "So can that bougie mansion in Tacoma."

"You don't like this season's shoot?"

"Not really," he admitted, turning to glance around the room. Kane let a slow smile move over his mouth when he spotted Kit, shooting her a nod before he went back to his beer. "Gotta make the studio happy."

"They pay the bills."

There was a small buzz working in the back of my head. I didn't want to be a full-on drunk while Gin was here, while Kane and Kit expected me not to be an embarrassment at least, so I took up slow sips, doing more holding of my Jack than actual drinking.

"Better than a real job," Kane offered, looking down at me when I only nodded. "You cool?" He didn't seem to like my shrug, gave me a tight frown, but he didn't comment until my cell started vibrating. "That's been happening a lot," he said, moving his head to my jacket when another text alert sounded.

I pulled it out long enough to set the ringer to vibrate.

"You got something brewing?"

I flicked a glance at him but didn't offer more than that in explanation. Truth of it was that something *was* brewing, but it wasn't a damn thing I'd share with Kane. Or anyone, for that matter.

It had been a good two weeks that my cell had gone off while we were filming or working on the reno of the Tacoma mansion. I ignored them all, because there wasn't a damn thing I'd do for Tony.

My kid brother had been a pain in my ass for most of my life. At least since my birth mother landed in prison for good and I got sent to my father and the family he had built with Nita, my stepmom. I'd been thirteen and a skinny white kid from East Texas living in the Lower Ninth Ward in New Orleans with my father and his new family. It was hell, fighting kids who didn't much appreciate or understand why my dad was white and Nita and my little brother and sister weren't. Kids can be fucking cruel. All the fights I got into defending my family, defending my place in that family, toughened me up. That neighborhood, that life we lived, did nothing for my kid brother. Tony had been coddled by our parents. I guess by me, too. I took the big-brother bullshit a little too seriously. Still, no way I was going to keep at that shit, no matter how many times he blew up my cell.

From behind us in the center of the bar, Kit's loud, exuberant laugh rang out. I followed Kane's gaze as he looked over his shoulder, staring at her again. There was something moving between them. Something that looked a lot like silent nagging. I recognized the subtle lift of her chin as she watched Kane and how he sucked at trying not to be obvious when he nodded a return.

The big man turned back, taking a long, slow pull of his beer before he cleared his throat. I wondered how long it had taken Kit to wrestle the storm Kane had been. Had it happened the second they'd been together? Or was it something she'd managed in the quiet, day-to-day while the rest of us lived our lives and ignored the specifics of Kit and Kane becoming a couple?

Whatever Kit's power, she wielded it then, making Kane fall in line with barely a twist of her head.

But that asshole took his time getting out whatever info Kit wanted him to relate.

"Listen, man..." he started, scratching the damp label on the neck of his bottle with his thumbnail. "Kit wanted me to... That is..."

I didn't much care about making people comfortable. Wasn't much the type to extract information when it got stuck in someone's throat. That wasn't going to change no matter how long it took Kane to organize his thoughts, string them into syllables, and push out the words those sounds became.

I had all night.

"I mean, you know how shit went crazy with Kiel and Cara's family with that asshole stalking her, you getting hurt, and then Gin leaving…"

I held the glass to my mouth, pausing to watch him over the rim. Had that bastard gone soft in the head? "I got a vague recollection."

My memory had gotten away from me, thanks to the anesthesia from the surgery, but I got the gist. That bastard stalking Cara attacked, pulled out a gun, and I took one in the gut.

Then, and only Christ knows why the hell I'd ever do this shit, Trudy had shown at the hospital, and I'd called her baby right in front of Gin. Repeatedly. I might not remember what happened exactly, but the fog was still lifting. Bits of it came back to me here and there, but fuck's sake, Kane was a dumbass if he thought I'd forget why Gin took off a few weeks after the shooting.

Kane's irritation seemed to bubble to the surface as he watched me sip my Jack long enough that he blew out a breath and scrubbed his face.

Figured I'd cut the man some slack. "Shit, man, just get it out."

"All right," he finally said, downing what remained of his beer before he turned to face me. "Gin's here."

I let my glance shoot across the bar, but I didn't linger on the sight of her. She chatted with Kit and the makeup women with a giant smile on her face. "Spotted that."

"She's...not alone."

That had my attention snapping back to Kane. But I had skills. I knew how to control my reaction. How to stay calm. How to funnel whatever bullshit I felt deep down.

Kane focused on me, eyes narrowed, mouth set into a tight expression that wasn't a smile. I got that he was hazarding a guess at how I'd react but didn't know what to make of how I went silent.

The whiskey didn't burn this time when I drank, pulling in twice the amount I had with my last sip. I needed it. It kept my jaw from working and the low, irritated grunt right in the center of my throat where it belonged. Inhaling, I shrugged, a stupid, half-assed attempt at indifference I was pretty sure Kane wouldn't buy.

"No need to walk on eggshells." When he remained quiet, I turned, narrowing my eyes as I scanned the crowd again. "Okay. So? Who's..."

"Um...Carelli. Johnny Carelli."

Kane couldn't see my face, something I was glad of. Carelli's name garnered the same reaction now as it had the day Kit told me about Gin's new gig.

Irritation.

Eyes slipping closed, I kept a tight hold on that threatening grunt, looking over the crowd and spotting that asshole as he relaxed against the bar. He leaned on an elbow, head tilted as he held court. Kit seemed oblivious to whatever the hell he said, but the makeup women, Neva and Lexi, were like groupies ready to throw their thongs right at his face.

"He's sponsoring a new crew for a show he wants to produce."

I cocked an eyebrow when Gin moved closer to him, a champagne flute held between her fingers and a half smile working over her full lips. She looked... bored? Or maybe that was my hope.

Maybe I was inventing shit that wasn't there and never would be.

"Thought Kiel said his in-laws were going legit."

"No," Kane said, motioning his empty beer at a waitress across the room. "He said his father-in-law was retiring. The Carellis will be working their hustles forever."

"And that includes renovation shows on cable?"

"They've got their hands in everything. Guess they wanna branch out."

I nodded, waving off the waitress when she handed Kane another beer and offered me a fresh Jack. Liquor wasn't what I wanted, not even when Gin stood closer to Johnny and the man leaned down, whispering something in her ear that made her blush.

"So..." Kane started, eyes going a little wide when I failed to hold back the low, frustrated grunt that left my throat. He stepped closer, tilting his head like he wanted a better look at me. "Man, you all right?"

Another grunt. This one coming when Gin let Carelli kiss her cheek. It tore me up to see that shit even though I hadn't done anything to prevent this. All this—her staying mad, her bolting the second the Portland gig came her way, her being here with Johnny *Fucking* Carelli, that was all on me.

It happened because I was a chickenshit.

It happened because I couldn't admit what I wanted.

It happened because I wasn't man enough to tell her how I felt.

"Yep," I finally answered Kane, grabbing my cell when it vibrated in my pocket. I didn't bother looking at the screen before I threw out a quick, "Gotta take this," to Kane and moved out onto the deck, answering the call just to give me something to distract myself from my brewing temper.

Didn't work just like I wanted it to.

"You got exactly thirty seconds before I hang up."

"Dale. Oh, thank God," Tony said. His voice was little more than a gravelly sound. That thick New Orleans accent was there—he'd never lose that if he could help it—and some part of me was glad. It made me a little homesick.

"Twenty-eight seconds."

"Man, I know. I know you think me calling is all bullshit. I know I've fucked up. I know it. But, Dale, you're my big brother..."

I spotted Gin grinning at some other bullshit Johnny said to her, and then the band kicked off their set. Carelli tugged her to the center of the dance floor, moving Gin around like she floated above the floor.

She let him.

That shit pissed me off.

"Oh, now I'm your big brother?" I asked Tony. I kept my attention on the dance floor and each torturous movement of Gin's supple, sweet body. "Wasn't your big brother when I tried putting your ass in rehab the four times..."

"I know that, man. I do, and I'm sorry..."

"Memory serves," I told Tony, nostrils flaring as Carelli rested his palm too damn low on Gin's back for my liking. "You told the DA the shit they caught you with was mine."

"Dale..."

"And I told you then I was done, didn't I?"

"Yeah, but this time..."

"Told you, little brother, that I was done saving your ass when you land in shit. I told you I wouldn't help you out again just so you could steal my shit and swipe my ATM card."

"Man, I know. I said I'm..."

Carelli bent low, whispering something right against Gin's ear that made her laugh loudly. Her fingers brushed against his face, and I knew then, no amount of Jack would keep me calm. Not even the training I had was going to help this week.

"All this shit, Tony, I've told you. I'm done with it. Gravy train has left the station."

"I'm...sick, Dale."

Something cold filled me up from the inside. It prickled and scratched in my chest when Tony spoke.

It made my blood run cold enough that I watched Gin and didn't see much of her. I saw my kid brother crying for me to help him as the NOPD led him away in handcuffs. I saw the wad of cash, *my* cash he'd stuffed in his shoe when he thought I wasn't looking, when he had two of the dealers he owed money to sucker-punch me in the gut and knock me against the dirty wall of the crack house I'd tracked Tony to.

Spent three days busted up in the hospital after that attack. *I'd* been sick then. I was sick now watching Carelli hold Gin, seeing how she didn't seem to hate the attention. That idea made me feel so nauseous that I almost missed the sound of Tony's hacking cough.

"How sick?"

"I just... I need to get clean, man."

I inhaled and shut my eyes to clear away the memory of Tony at nine. He tried like hell to keep up with me when we played a game of touch football with Nita's brothers in a city park. He'd been a scrawny thing but held his own. I'd respected his hustle.

"Please, Dale. I...I need to not be sick." I heard the sharp inhale he took and braced myself. I knew what was coming before he said a word. It was the buildup he always used. The plea he thought I couldn't refuse. "If you can come get me...maybe let me dry out on your sofa. Maybe...I dunno, man, are there good places there in Seattle?"

"There might be," I told him, fingers squeezing my cell when Gin looked up, her gaze right on me as I held that phone against my ear. There was a lot she said in that look. It was the slip of emotion I spotted as she watched me. How she looked like she didn't know if she wanted to hate me or forgive me one more time.

I could relate to the emotion.

Tony had done a lot to hurt me.

I'd done a lot to hurt Gin just by never giving her what we both wanted.

The thin lines of love and hate, of stubbornness and forgiveness, get thinner when you start lying to yourself.

I'd done that for years.

"I'm not in the second chances game anymore, little brother." Gin stared at me a half second longer before she blinked, pulling her focus from me. Something snapped inside my head. Something that had me forgetting that I once knew how to forgive.

"Dale, please. There's something I have to...just. Please, bro." The plea in his voice made me frown, but it didn't take away the memory of all the times he'd lied for a fix or robbed me blind to get it. "Haven't you ever done anything you regret? Haven't you ever had to beg for forgiveness?"

I hadn't. Not once, but as Gin let Carelli dance her away from the window, his arm tight against her waist, I thought it might be time I started.

Chapter Two
Gin

Damn. This would be easier if Dale looked like shit. A little paunch around the middle, maybe a double chin that hadn't been there when I left Seattle, that might have done enough to keep me from watching him through the busy crowd.

"You good, *bella*?" Johnny rubbed the tip of one finger down my bare bicep.

"I'm good."

He took that reassurance and nodded toward the waitress he'd been trying to call over for ten minutes. I grinned as he hustled away from me, weaving through the wave of people crowding the bar in search of another rum and Coke. I took the opportunity to breathe.

And to not look at Dale for the thirtieth time.

He'd always been beautiful. Always seemed ready to rebel against any military standards the second he was able and wore his hair on the long side—black as coal and just touching his jaw. It was a little longer than it had been a year ago and flopped a bit on top, but he kept it neat, pushed off his face, and clean. There was more scruff around his angular, square-jawed features, but it suited him. A little too damn much.

The son of a bastard had put on a good twenty pounds of solid muscle. It showed in his trim waist, accentuated by the tailored jacket and dark jeans he wore. Just a small curve of his defined chest could be spotted through Dale's white, open-collar button-up, and he stood outside on the balcony, expression hard, jaw flexing as he watched me while Johnny moved me around the dance floor.

Utterly unfair for him to be that beautiful.

"We see you looking," Neva said when I stood next to her and Lexi.

The women had spent most of the past hour fawning over Johnny, asking him the most inappropriate questions.

"*Is* The Godfather *based on anyone in your family?*"

"*Are you a* made *man?*"

"*Is it true what they say about Italian men?*"

That one, he answered.

"Yes, ladies," Johnny promised, taking both their hands in his to kiss their knuckles, gaze moving between each of their shocked, blushing faces as he held them. "We're exceptionally well hung and fantastic lovers."

"What do you think I see?" I asked, ignoring the grin Neva wore as she stood at my side, watching the crowd like a lioness scoping out which antelope looked like the easiest mark.

"Dale *Hot Damn* Hunter."

"Yes, indeed," Lexi agreed.

It was impossible to ignore the pair as they watched Dale. Their attention quiet but focused as he left the balcony and walked ten feet away, passing women in his wake who stopped and watched him.

No one was immune to the sight of him. From Kit's approving nod as he winked at her, to Cara, who was heavily pregnant but, apparently, not remotely blind. Each low mutter of "'scuse me" and gentle brush of elbows and arms, every weave of his wide, angular body through the crowd caught attention.

Dale, though, didn't seem to notice anyone but the bartender when he motioned for another drink.

"Keto and hot yoga," Neva said, the last word elevated.

"Girl, hell no. CrossFit." Lexi's assertion came out on a wistful sigh.

"Maybe," Neva answered, head tilted toward her friend.

Dale nodded a thanks to the bartender and turned to face the crowd, his eyebrows shooting up when a group of gawking women quickly turned away from him. They were all caught staring and clearly embarrassed that they had been too. Dale seemed to take the attention in stride, inhaling behind his drink.

"Or it could be the influence of all those hot Navy friends of his he's been hanging around."

"What Navy friends?" I asked.

When I lived in the city, none of Dale's SEAL brothers were here. They were either still deployed or living in other parts of the country.

"Whole big group of them, half a dozen or so," Lexi said, turning to smile at me like the thought of a group of Navy SEALs made her happier than a two-for-one sale at Sephora. "Big bunch of them went off active and relocated. The ones who can make it all meet up at this new gym out off 1st Ave."

"Belltown," Neva clarified. "At least, that's what Asher said anyhow."

"Asher?" I asked.

"Oh, that little intern has gotten his shit together. He listens now." Lexi nodded to a couple making their way to the bar.

The pair moved closer, and I stepped away to give them room to order a drink when the waitress near us changed direction and they missed their chance for a refill.

"Asher runs between Dale and Kane on set, gophering things for them or filling in when someone on the crew is sick. Anyway, Asher told Lydia, *our* intern, that Dale leaves the set every afternoon and heads for the gym. I've seen him first thing in the morning running the trail around the development where we're shooting. That man just doesn't stay put."

For as long as I'd known him, Dale always kept himself up. It was never with anything quite so focused as being in a gym. He liked being outdoors, kayaking or running trails, sometimes mountain climbing. Always something that kept him outside. He never overworked himself. If he was doing that now, it was for a distraction.

Unable to help myself, I glanced at him as Kane stood next to him. Dale nodded when Kane spoke, shrugging now and then, but otherwise not speaking. That had changed too.

Dale had always been quiet but never rude. He'd never been closed-lipped, and sometimes that bothered the hell out of me.

"Whatever the hell he's doing," Neva said with her attention back on Dale, "damn if it ain't paying off. Look at him. I mean, *Lord*!"

That last word came out loud enough that several people turned, catching more stares than I guess Neva had expected, but the makeup artist loved the attention. I did not.

Dale turned as well, watching Neva and Lexi as the two women laughed among themselves, then shifted his gaze to me. As he looked me over, his features shifting and softening, his mouth quirking into something resembling a smile, my heart sped up quick.

I wanted to hate him. I'd managed to do that very thing for the past year, but it was exhausting and damn near impossible when he looked at me the way he did then. The same way he looked at me the night at Kane and Kiel's cabin, right before the damn fool got himself shot and everything fell apart.

Dale kept his thoughts guarded, locked down tight. You only knew what he was thinking when he clued you in. I guessed he was shifting between being maybe not so irritated to see me, possibly a little miffed that I'd taken off for Portland and didn't say goodbye, and what, to me, looked like a touch anxious for a conversation I damn sure wasn't ready to have with him. Especially not when a wave of lust flushed my skin as the memory hit me of Dale kneeling in front of me, his mouth over my throbbing pussy, his grip greedy and tight. I managed not to let it overwhelm me, though I had to keep my attention away from the man in question.

From the corner of my eye, I noticed Dale taking a step toward me. That small, twitching half smile dropped when I left the bar. I maneuvered through the crowd, hoping to get enough people between my ex-best friend and me. But Dale moved faster than I did, his movements stealthy and slick. He knew how to bypass stragglers. How to avoid drunk, sloppy dancers when they managed to get in my way.

I was nearly to the balcony when I spotted his reflection just behind me. That tall, looming frame like a shadow at my back.

"Gingerbre..." He stopped himself, swallowing down the nickname before it fully left his mouth.

It hurt to hear, but I pushed that sting down. Just like I had all my memories of Dale. All the good and bad I tried to tell myself I had to forget about. There was no future in a past with roots so firmly planted in yesterday. Dale's past would never leave him, and he had no interest in tomorrow.

The last time I saw him, he ran from his truck and into my Craftsman bungalow. It took more strength than I thought I had to watch him tear through that empty house trying to stop me from leaving. But I was already gone. I'd been gone the second I realized he could never tell me what I needed to hear from him.

The moment I knew he'd go on pretending nothing had happened between us that night in the cabin.

But now, I had no choice. I had to face him. Tomorrow afternoon, I'd stand at his side, practicing walking down the aisle. The day after that, we'd do it for real. I couldn't pretend I hated him anymore. I couldn't go on lying to either of us.

He stepped back when I turned, dropping his hand to his side. I held my breath, wishing I'd kept lying to myself, kept pretending. Jaw tight, lips parted a fraction, Dale moved his gaze over my face like he wanted to check for himself if I'd changed. Each glance he made over my features told him he marked the differences, like he wondered if there were new lines on my face, maybe a new color in my hair.

There weren't any.

Nothing had changed.

And everything had.

I looked right back, spotted one or two grays around his temples that hadn't been there before. It suited him. The scruff on his chin was still all black, and his handsome face, though rugged, was mildly weathered. He was still perfectly imperfect.

Damn.

He was even more beautiful two feet away from me.

"Gin," he said, nodding. It was an inflection I recognized as Dale's nervous tone. He used it when he was unsure of himself, something he rarely was. Something I'd only heard from him twice in all the years I'd known him.

"Dale." My tone was no better than his. I swallowed, hoping that whatever nerves had stuck in my throat would get dislodged before I spoke again.

It was awkward and unusual to be standing in front of him. I had a million thoughts. A million wishes and not one sentence to string together. Not the slightest pulse of courage to let any of those things come out. I still wanted to hit him. And kiss him. And tell him I missed him. And tell him he hurt me. And tell him I had to move on.

Mainly, I wanted to stay angry.

Just then, right in that small moment, for reasons that made no sense at all, I wanted to cradle my irrational anger and let it warm me. It was what had held me up since I'd left for Portland. It shouldn't have mattered that seeing Dale had wrecked my resolve inside of ten minutes. I still wanted to hold on to that familiar anger.

"How..." He cleared his throat like he didn't like the way his voice had cracked. Like he wasn't sure who'd just tried speaking for him before he tried again. "You all right?"

"I'm good." I let that anger circle back. Let it stiffen my spine a bit, keeping me from relaxing too much around him. "You?"

Dale looked me over again. This time, his appraisal was slower, calculating, like he knew what I was doing and just looking long enough, hard enough would fracture whatever anger I used to keep myself protected. Gaze working over my face as I stared off to the side, pretending to look for Kit or Cara or even Johnny, my date. Dale went on watching me, his attention like a laser scanning over my body, examining, appraising until I had to look back.

Dale squinted, his features hardening before he licked his lips, as though something had occurred to him and he found it funny. "Yeah. I'm making it." He stepped closer, head tilted to the side because, I guessed, he knew that sweet, half-smile, head-tilt thing he did affected me. He'd used it a hundred times to get his way from me. Dale might be a grizzled SEAL who lacked social graces, but when he wanted something, he knew how to get it. He was best at getting me to agree to things I'd never believed possible.

It shocked me to see him using that little gesture less than ten minutes into our conversation. If he came any closer to me, grinned any sweeter, I was sure all recollection of why I'd left Seattle in the first place would shoot right out of my head.

"What?" I finally said. He'd planted a small smile over his mouth. Something I'd rarely seen from him. I couldn't help moving my gaze down at his full glass, internally musing how many Jacks he'd downed. Dale always was extra flirty when Jack came to visit.

"Three," he answered the question I didn't ask, forcing my attention back at his face.

"I didn't..."

"Written on every inch of that pretty mug of yours," he said, waving his finger around my face. It was meant as a tease. I knew Dale well enough to understand his ribbing. He was good at that, with me at least. "But it's only been three, and as you know, I can handle plenty more of my buddy Jack than three."

"Nearly a bottle, if memory serves," I said, unable to help the laugh that bubbled from my throat at the memory of Dale the night of his birthday the year after Trudy left him. He was in nothing but his cowboy boots and boxer briefs, a bottle of Gentleman Jack between his fingers as he serenaded my block, promising the world there were no other women in the world like "New Orleans Ladies."

It was the single most god-awful out-of-tune song I'd ever heard. At least he was able to hold his liquor long enough for me to find his jeans, which he'd abandoned on the front porch, and tuck him in on my sofa.

He'd been beautiful, harmless, so lost. All I'd wanted to do was help my friend through the grief of betrayal his cheating wife had caused. We tried liquor. We tried raw honesty. We tried a hell of a lot of laughter and then...well.

Shit.

Another wave of lust collected from my memories shot forward. I stepped back, cursing myself for almost letting Dale charm me into forgetting why I had to leave Seattle. Not once had he mentioned that night at the cabin. No amount of trips down memory lane would make up for the fact that Dale clearly wanted to forget what we'd done and what he'd almost said to me.

His grin faded when I stepped back, remembering the hurt that still lingered in my chest every time I thought about him. The crowd rushed the dance floor and I watched them, fighting the urge to face Dale and the need to reach out to him.

"I'm...glad you're doing okay." He moved his hand. His fingers coming inches from my wrist, but I pretended not to notice and curled my arms in front of my chest. I couldn't let him think I was his friend. It was too soon to be too familiar. He didn't get that from me anymore. Not ever again. That's what I told myself. "Look, I've got to..." I was almost clear, breaking free, proving to myself that I could walk away and he would not affect me...

Two steps. A twist of my head, a low, swift breath. That's all I managed.

One.

Two.

And then Dale grabbed my wrist, turned me back, held me right in front of him.

"I've got things to say."

I opened my mouth, ready to tell him not to bother. He'd said something similar to me before, then pretended he hadn't. I wasn't going to fall for it twice.

But Dale stopped me, eyes tightening so that I could barely make out the black irises, teeth clenching like he anticipated every scenario and had a response for each one. The tease was gone from his expression, as though he'd never attempted it. "You let me say them, and I swear, I'll be done. I won't hassle you. I won't get in..." He glanced over my shoulder, those eyes opening, shifting, and the hard line of his mouth tightened. "I won't get in your way."

I turned to my right, spotting Johnny near the bar, his smile easy but his eyes curious. A little interested and on alert. He relaxed when I shook my head, waving him off.

"What things do you have to say to me, Dale?" I asked, prepared to dismiss him.

He didn't seem ready for that. "Things I can't say in the middle of a crowd with Johnny *Fuckin'* Carelli looking at me like he wants to jump me." Dale let my wrist go but didn't step away from me. "Tomorrow. Nine o'clock, if you can make it. Meet me at Riley's on 1st." Some of the tightness in his face relaxed.

I could smell the whiskey on his breath, and it made me a little drunk. He licked his lips again, and I inhaled, hating that I liked the smell and the way it came off him. Hating that some part of me wanted to see how drunk I could get off the taste of Dale Hunter.

He exhaled and I closed my eyes, suppressing a shiver when he leaned forward to kiss my cheek, and that sweet whiskey smell gave me a contact high. "This...this is me saying please."

Chapter Three
Gin

Hell, could that man could make an entrance. He was never late.

It had to be a throwback to all those years being up before dawn, on deployment doing whatever the hell it was SEALs did that none of us are ever supposed to know about. But Dale's place was off the 522 right where a dump truck had spilled ten yards of cedar mulch.

You hit that mess on the 522? I'd texted him.

I did. At the light across the street. Be there in forty seconds.

I figured that would put him behind me, but Dale was always prepared and rarely caught by surprise. I parked my Charger in the spot closest to the front of the small diner just a minute after nine. At 9:02

exactly, the familiar roar of his motorcycle thundering down 1st Avenue sounded just as I started away from my car. Dale moved his bike down the street with ease, driving it up the inclined driveway with one hand and gliding into the spot next to my Charger before I could get my hand on the front door.

Ridiculous. Utterly damn ridiculous to look that cool. That polished in a pair of jeans and a simple black leather jacket. He was off his bike, helmet tucked under his arm, and his gloved hand on the door handle before I had time to open it.

I'd always been a little dumbstruck by Dale. I'd told myself a year had been long enough to help me forget what kind of man I'd let myself fall for. Behind the guise of being his right-hand woman on set, I could watch him without needing an excuse. I could see how the man worked. See a side of him no one else got to witness, and it was always a hell of a show.

He slipped off that bike like it was nothing. Like it was easier to maneuver that 500-pound Indian than a toddler manning a Big Wheel. He shoved one hand through his hair, and all those thick, beautiful waves stayed right where he'd pushed them. God alive. That was just Dale. He moved, and things just sort of stayed put. I'd forgotten what it was like.

I'd forgotten the control he had.

I'd forgotten how much being around him could make me forget what I wanted.

All the things I knew he'd never give me.

It took me a second to snap myself from the daze as he joined me at the entrance. When he nodded toward the door, opening it wide, I straightened my shoulders and brushed past him without a greeting or anything more welcoming than a jerk of my chin.

The diner was small, the morning crowd thinning out. We'd eaten at this place two, maybe three times before. Enough to know that five to eight a.m. was the peak morning breakfast rush. That much I remembered from our Seattle locations.

Dale nodded to the hostess when she threw him a wink and pointed to a booth set at the back of the diner, beyond the front counter. There was no one around this section because the lighting was dimmer, and the back window had a busted set of blinds that hung at an angle in the center of the glass.

Dale waited for me to sit, and I slid across the bench, watching him. He took off his gloves and tucked them into his helmet and stored both at his side while the waitress hurried over to set two empty mugs in front of us.

"Coffee?" she asked, offering the steaming aluminum pot in her hand.

"Thanks," I said, nodding to Dale's mug out of habit.

He waited for the woman to place two laminated menus in front of us and leave before he spoke, looking at the broken blinds, eyebrows moving up. "This booth suits me. It's cold. No sunlight. Nobody wants to sit in the cold."

I shivered, pulling my own coat tighter around my neck. "No one but you."

The question came out like an accusation, a little sharp, a lot bitchy, enough that the half smile that had twitched on Dale's mouth died in an instant. I didn't apologize. It wasn't a lie. He never wanted company, except for me or Kane and, maybe on his good days, Kit. It was no surprise to me he'd pick a spot in an emptying diner that no one wanted to be in. The coolest, dimmest spot in the place.

"Guess so." He sipped his black coffee, thumb smoothing against the handle.

Then he went quiet on me, only showing any reaction in his expressions when his cell vibrated in his pocket or the waitress came by to ask for our order.

"Just coffee for me," I told her, shaking my head when Dale opened his mouth to argue.

The waitress returned to the counter, mumbling something under her breath. I grabbed a creamer, fully aware that Dale watched as I added more to my coffee, likely wondering if we were going to sit here all morning not speaking. Curious if the other would ever utter a sound.

"You're not hungry?" He stacked my empty creamer containers into each other while I stirred sugar into my mug.

"No. Kit and I had a little too much tequila last night, and my stomach can't take more than coffee and toast."

He lifted his hand, as though he were trying to get the waitress's attention. I grabbed his wrist, and the quick flash of contact made Dale jerk his gaze to me.

"It's fine, really." I pulled my hand back, squeezing my fingers together. "Not really up to eating anything yet."

"You need something in your stomach." His suggestion reminded me of Thanksgiving two years ago when I got the flu. I thought I'd spend the holiday alone, puking my guts out. Dale had been the only one to check up on me. It had been so out of our norm for him to stay and look after me, missing out on Kit's amazing rosemary turkey spread to nurse me back to life. Usually, it was me playing nursemaid while Dale got shitty. But that day, I saw a side of him that had surprised me. It was surfacing just a bit right now as he affected the same, not-at-all-like-him tone. "You'll end up passing out or..."

I stared out of the half-obscured window, trying to clear away the memory of that Thanksgiving Day. Dale with my feet in his lap as he watched the game. That was a lifetime ago. Now, I didn't need Dale's concern. It was wasted on me, and I sensed he understood my feeling.

Dale pushed his mug away from himself and scrubbed a hand over his face before he cleared his throat. "Fuck, I feel like a frog on a hot plate."

I just couldn't help myself. Despite the tension, despite the awkwardness of the situation, a loud, uncontrollable laugh blurted from my throat. "What the hell?"

Dale grinned, his shoulders relaxing as he waved me off. He hazarded one long, slow look my way before he shook his head. He seemed to give up any pretenses that, like me, he wasn't a nervous wreck.

"This ain't us."

It wasn't. We both knew it. I watched Dale watching me. We'd never been the type of people who walked on eggshells around each other. We were now.

"No," I finally said, ignoring that small, nagging voice in the back of my head that reminded me of the hurt Dale had dealt me. "This ain't us."

He paused, rubbing his fingers over his mouth. He looked out of the window, giving a clear view of that perfect, symmetrical profile. It was just damn criminal for a man to be that beautiful.

"Used to be...there wasn't a thing I couldn't say, in my own way, to you," he said, still watching the traffic outside the diner. "But then..." He squeezed his eyes shut, scrubbing his nails through his scruff like he couldn't finish the thought he'd started. Then Dale waved it off, blowing out a breath before he glanced at me. "There's a lot we left unsaid. A lot I got to answer for and I know that. But just now I wanna say that it's a shitshow with you not around. The set has gone to hell."

"The show?" I said, not surprised that Dale was deflecting.

"And...that dumb little tree you bought me is turning brown."

I blinked at him, questioning the sanity of my surprise that Dale had managed the impossible. "It's an aloe plant, Dale. Who the hell kills an aloe vera plant?"

"Didn't say it was dead...it's just..."

"What are you saying?"

He curled a napkin between his fingers, flaring his nostrils as though he didn't want to say the one thing he knew he had to get out. "Well, I suppose that... everything has gone to shit."

"You mentioned that." I leaned back, trying not to laugh at the way he drummed his fingers against the table. He was nervous and Dale Hunter wasn't the type of man to ever be truly nervous. "The set and the aloe...because?"

He jerked his gaze to me. I spotted the tension working in his jaw as Dale gritted his teeth. "Because," he started, releasing a long sigh. "You aren't there."

His stare felt like a burn against my skin. It was weighted and searing. I closed my eyes, inhaling deeply. Nothing had been resolved between us. We'd walked away from each other—Dale every time he teased me with improbable maybes; and me when I left Seattle with no promise of ever coming back.

I took away my friendship. He took away my hope.

"No," I said, not meaning to make my voice as soft as it came out. "I'm not there."

He knew why I left.

He had to know why I planned to stay gone.

"I never meant..." He didn't finish. Whatever excuse Dale had ready for me got swallowed up by the chirping alert of his cell. Whoever it came from hardened his features. Another heavy exhale and Dale rubbed his face, looking tired, deflated.

"You sleeping?" I couldn't help asking.

"A little." "You need to take care of yourself."

Dale leaned against the table, his features relaxing as he watched me. "See, that's another thing that's gone to shit. Don't have you here to nag me about eating three squares or getting enough protein."

"You look like you've been managing okay in that department." It was a compliment I should have kept to myself, one that put a stupid grin on Dale's face I equally loved and hated.

"Is that right?" He leaned back, stretching one arm across the back of the bench behind him. "Been looking, have you?" When I rolled my eyes, Dale continued, and that grin widened. "Go ahead, I won't pick on you if you admit it."

"You're full of yourself."

"You're the one talking about me looking good." He winked at me then, taking hold of my hand when I gave his hand a light slap. There was a small current of electricity that shot from the tips of his fingers to my wrist when he grazed his fingers across my knuckles. Dale dropped the smile from his face but didn't move his touch from my hand. "Truth is, Gingerbread, I've missed you a lot."

God, I'd missed him too, and I wanted to tell him. I wanted to touch him back, take his hand and hold it against my palm. I wanted to feel the heat of his skin on mine. It was tempting, like the sweetest, most decadent drug taunting an addict.

"So many times, I've thought about you...and me... and everything that could have happened and never did. About what *could* happen in the future."

It felt like a gut punch. Something stinging. Something that hurt so badly I didn't think I'd be able to walk away from this table with my head held up. How could he say nothing happened? How could he dismiss what he'd done to me? What he'd said?

Dale's frown came slow, in small segments as I sat up, pulling my hand into my lap. I saw his disappointment as the seconds ticked by, but I didn't speak. He went quiet. I wondered what he thought, if he believed how he touched me, teased me could be so easy to forget.

When I couldn't take his stare, when the air around us had grown too thick with awkward tension, I turned and stared right at him, holding back my surprise at the look of worry and disappointment on Dale's face. It wasn't going to work. I was the master of those disappointed looks. I'd given them to him a hundred times. He never understood that he was the reason they stayed etched on my face.

Blowing out a breath, I leaned forward and moved my cooling coffee to the side. "The problem with that is, things are different."

Dale's bottom eyelid pulsed. A small twitch that told me he was irritated. He recovered, copying my position by leaning forward. "Nothing is different."

His hands were inches from mine. He could stretch his fingers and graze my knuckles again, take back what I kept from him. He wouldn't. That wasn't his style. In fact, the thought would likely never occur to him. He wouldn't face even the remotest possibility of rejection. Just like the idea that I had changed. He didn't see it. He never would.

I rested against the booth, arms crossed. "*Everything* is different."

"You still take two creams and two sugars in your coffee."

"Dale."

"You still like bourbon in your sweet tea?" He shifted in his seat, the booth squeaking as he flatted his hand against the table. "You still get scared when you watch *The Conjuring*? You still like thunderstorms? Nothing's changed except the distance."

"*I've* changed!" My voice was loud, punctuated by the slap of my hand against the table.

Dale sat up, hardening his features.

I hadn't meant to lose my temper. I hadn't meant to let him see what effect he had on me, but God knows, if anyone could get under my skin, it was Dale.

Outside the window, two cop cars zipped by, their lights flashing and sirens silent as they led a black limo through the streets.

I went over the list of curses I'd prepared to shout at Dale. All the rude and insulting names I'd wanted to call him. But just then, I didn't have the energy.

Dale kept quiet and folded his arms across his large chest, his expression shifting from surprised to soft worry. He covered his mouth with his fingers as he watched me, ignoring the constant vibration of his phone; watched and waited for an explanation he had to know I wanted to make.

I obliged, shooting my gaze from my folded hands in front of me on the table to his face. When I spoke, my voice was level. "What I'll accept has changed, and I'm not gonna go back."

Another vibration from his cell and I wondered why Dale ignored it. It could have been his SEAL brothers. He always answered for them. It could have been his kid sister back home in New Orleans. It could have been Kane, but something told me Dale knew who had been calling. He knew and made a point not to answer.

"You know, if I was different... If things were..." He looked down, shifting in his seat, looking uncomfortable, like his jacket had suddenly grown too small for him.

Dale wasn't good at apologies. He wasn't good at talking, not about stuff that mattered. He was so scared by it that he hadn't even mentioned what might have happened if no one had shown up to pick a fight at the cabin. That's why we were here. I'd gotten tired of waiting for him to stop making excuses. I was tired of those improbable maybes.

"If I was...different..."

"But you're not, and you know it."

I couldn't hear it. Not again. The excuses never changed. They hadn't when he'd banged on my door after he left the hospital, begging for me to take care of him. They hadn't when I'd spotted him and Trudy on the set the day he returned to work. They hadn't when he'd left drunk messages on my cell after I'd left for Portland. They wouldn't now.

He opened his mouth but didn't speak.

My head shake kept him from doling out another excuse that wouldn't matter. "You aren't going to be who you can't be. You aren't going to..."

I wouldn't do it for him.

Couldn't.

I'd helped Dale through a lot of his shit.

I'd been his best friend, but I had to draw the line.

For my own damn sanity, I had to draw the line somewhere.

"It...tore me up." The words left his mouth in a bundle, a rush of syllables that were sounds through a long breath. Dale's features twisted, and the indistinct lines around his eyes deepened. The frustration and exhaustion taking over his face as though he'd rather punch something than say what was on his mind. When his cell vibrated again, he silenced it, holding it in his left hand as he spoke. "That day. You were gone. I went to your place, and you were just...gone. You just... You left. Me."

Another ring. This one immediately going off again the second Dale silenced it. I knew who it was and why Dale was so adamant about not taking the call. He didn't fight me when I jerked the phone from his hand, but he did hold his breath. He watched me as I read Trudy's name and the local number across the screen.

Holy hell.

A year later and that evil cow was still in the picture.

"Yeah, well, tore me up to hear you call that bitch your wife again." I threw his phone at him, and he caught it. "Guess we're even now." I ignored him as he called after me, throwing a ten onto the counter as I left.

Trudy could have him.

I was done with Dale Hunter for good.

Chapter Four
Dale

Didn't much see a point in weddings.

Hell, I didn't much see a point in marriage, but then, it was that attitude that left me sitting on my own yesterday morning as Gin marched right out of the diner.

Fucking Trudy.

I swear to Christ, my ex-wife was a cancer that had no damn cure. She'd shown up last year when I'd landed in the hospital after some mafia asshole didn't get the hint that Kiel's woman didn't want him.

I'd been protecting the people I cared about, Gin among them. Hopped up on morphine, I forgot myself and went all moony and stupid when Trudy showed up.

That had started all sorts of hell with Gin.

It had taken all of six hours for me to cut that devil loose once the meds wore off.

"You can't leave," she'd told me. Her ironed scrubs and hospital badge without a spot on them, like always. Told me enough that Trudy probably still wasn't much of a fan of hard work, even at her nursing job.

"I got it covered."

"But I thought we... I mean, you and me..."

She hadn't taken too kindly to how loudly I'd laughed in her face, but it got her away from me. It cut her loose of whatever hold she was angling to have on me again. Took a threat against her freedom and her daddy to finally be rid of her. That and security on the set to ban her. Woman just couldn't get the point, but even that didn't keep Gin from leaving.

Had no clue why Trudy was blowing up my phone again. Or why in God's name Gin had to see that nonsense right when I was working up the nerve to spill some heavy shit to her.

She wasn't interested in what I had to say.

Not if the way she was carrying on told me anything, and fuck me, it did.

If I was being honest, I couldn't fault Carelli or any man for wanting Gin. She was beautiful, that was true enough, and I'd know. Women all over the world were beautiful. I'd been to enough places. Seen enough of them to say for sure that every part of the world had beauty. I'd seen exotic Sudanese women with flawless onyx skin and luscious mouths. Nordic women with hair the color of straw and eyes like ice. I'd seen Colombian women with thick, corkscrew hair and skin the color of a fawn. Welsh women with pale, smooth, alabaster skin and hair the color of a gun barrel. All were beautiful. All had held my notice, kept it for a while, but none had taken hold of me like Gin.

None had ever made me think there could be another chance, a life outside of the disaster I'd made for myself.

It had been subtle. So subtle I hadn't realized what was happening until it was too late—asleep on my sofa with my best friend curled up next to me and an old Clint Eastwood movie playing in the background. She wasn't hard edges then. She was calm, cool, and at peace. I'd try to shake off the growing attraction, even though I'd caught on to how she felt a solid year before I'd had similar thoughts, but it just wouldn't go away. With Gin's body leaning against mine, I felt something I'd never once felt in my life—peace.

Now, I couldn't even get her to look at me. I didn't have a single idea how to change that shit either. She'd avoided looking at me for longer than ten minutes since she'd left the diner yesterday morning. She didn't bother saying much at the rehearsal or at the wedding tonight.

I knew time was slipping away from me.

She danced in the middle of the banquet hall, place stupid with folks dressed in monkey suits and fancy dresses to celebrate Kane and Kit's wedding. The music was loud, the food was abundant, and the women were beautiful. But the only one who held my attention was the redhead in the middle of the dance floor laughing with her friends, her hands over her head as the music thumped and beat my senses like a fucking drum. This wasn't where I wanted to be, but I couldn't move from my spot. Not with Gin twisting and shimmying the way she was, looking as beautiful as she did.

She and Cara had their hair up. Cara was pregnant. Looked beautiful and glowed. She fit the Grecian goddess theme both women had going with the dresses Kit picked for her bridesmaids. But the gold color suited Gin better.

Where Cara's round belly protruded and made her look like some sort of fertility goddess, Gin's hugged her breasts, dipped low, showed off what I'd only guessed she had going on under all her T-shirts and flannels she preferred to wear on set. It did something to my head watching her. Being this close to her, seeing her like I never had before, I realized I'd underestimated everything I thought I knew about her.

"You know, Hunter, I can't blame you."

Johnny Carelli didn't know shit about me. He might have learned what he could from Kiel. Maybe he had people who could find out a thing or two, but there wasn't enough money—no amount of mob money anyway—to get my file. He stood next to me, his elbow grazing my forearm as we both watched Gin dancing with her friends. It took effort not to sock him in the jaw.

"She's *bella*. Sweet. Smart."

"Plenty of beautiful, sweet, smart women for you in New York, Carelli." I didn't bother to look at him when he nodded. I could make out his grin and quick shrug. "Maybe you should go back there and find one for yourself." I turned, hating to break my appraisal of Gin, but I needed this asshole to see my face, to see the threat in my eyes when I made it.

He watched me, holding up a finger when one of his men stepped to his side. "Easy, Angelo," he told the guy before he looked up at me. "Hunter and I are just having a conversation."

"That what we're doing?"

Carelli moved the ice around in his glass, gaze slipping to the dance floor before he looked at me again. His mouth held an easy smile I knew he didn't mean. "It's true. New York has plenty of beautiful women. Plenty to keep me company, and if I'm lucky, that'll include our favorite redhead." He lifted his glass to Gin, offering her a smile.

There was an uneasy grin on her face when I glanced at her, like she didn't understand why I was standing in front of Carelli and what we had to say to each other. But then Kit pulled Gin away from the dance floor, shoving her bouquet into her hand as they moved toward the bandstand and Kit landed in

Kiel's lap. Kane knelt in front of her, trying to get at her garter under her skirts.

"That's not Gin," I told Carelli, looking away from the crowd. The threat itched on my tongue, ready to come out in a whip of anger and curses to make this asshole understand I wasn't fucking around. "If you had any idea about her, you'd know she doesn't do well in the city."

"She's done well in Portland, heading her own crew for the network." Carelli handed his man his glass and took a step. He didn't touch me but was close enough to put me on alert.

"Portland ain't New York, not by a mile." I came closer too, hands in my pockets, irritated when I remembered I wore a stupid suit and not my jeans and boots. It would be easy to trounce this asshole if I weren't worried about losing traction in these stupid shoes.

"Maybe not." His eyebrows moved together as the crowd at our side began a countdown. "But that won't stop me from offering her a spot on the new rehab show I'm producing. She'll be great at it, and it will give her opportunities Portland can't." He leaned forward, and he ran his gaze over my face. "It'll give her opportunities nothing or nobody on the West Coast can give her."

There was a roar from the crowd, a lot of squealing laughter, and I had to remind myself I couldn't fight this bastard in the middle of my boss's wedding. It wouldn't look good in front of the network bigwigs sitting at two tables across the room. Plus, I didn't much care for the idea of Kane or, hell, worse than him, Kit threatening my balls if I ruined their wedding reception.

Carelli's stare shifted, his eyes moving to the right, over my head, and then something slapped against my neck. I jerked a hand up, not taking my gaze from his smug grin.

"Congratulations." He nodded at the fabric I grabbed as I pulled it off my shoulder. "Looks like you're next." Then the asshole walked away.

I stood there holding Kit's blue silk garter between my slack fingers.

Chapter Five
Dale

"Well, I'm gonna miss you." Kit was a little drunk. Her words came out as if they'd been lodged in her throat. She leaned on Gin like her feet could use a break. But I caught the frown she wore and the way she looked on the verge of tears.

The place was dark, the crowd thick, but even I, dense as I was sometimes, could make out a teary-eyed woman when I spotted one. But Kit's tears and the pause in her wedding day glee wasn't what had my throat knotting up.

"You can visit me, you know," Gin said, talking over the music still pulsing around the reception hall. "New York is just a plane ride away."

That did it.

Throat knotted, stomach gurgling, chest twisting like a broken Slinky.

"It's just so...so quick." Kit led Gin closer to the door.

I stood inside it, against the wall in the lobby, doing my best to catch the breeze from the half-open door. Shit was stuffy in that hall and stupid with women who had gotten more annoying the longer the night went on. Liquor made inhibitions fly right out the window, and Neva had downed about six of those pink drinks in the champagne flutes. That woman had a strong grip for someone so tiny.

"I know. It's crazy, right?" Gin said, reminding me that she was leaving and doing it quickly. "But I gotta go, don't I? I need to move on from..."

"Everything?" Kit asked.

"Yeah. Everything." There was a little too much breath in that answer. Too much meaning that I worried was wrapped up in me and my bullshit.

Shit. Carelli wasted no time. I glanced into the hall, scanning the room for that bastard, spotting him dancing with Lexi in the middle of the dance floor. Good. That might buy me some time. She'd had two more of those drinks than Neva, as far as I spotted.

Gin nodded to Kit as the bride was pulled away from her, and the redhead slipped into the hallway. I took my chance, following behind Gin. Had no clue what I might do or how I'd handle myself, but I had to say something. Had to at least try. The way Carelli was moving, he'd probably pack her up and have her on the next flight to New York, and then where would I be?

She headed toward the ladies' room, greeting several members of the crew as she passed them, then stopped in the middle of the hall when Asher and his girl Lydia spotted me.

"Dale, hey, man," the kid said, looking away from Gin to wave at me.

"Bowtie," I greeted, sticking with the nickname Kane had given him when he showed up on set sporting suspenders and a damn bow tie—hipster bullshit that the kid had thankfully retired. The nickname stuck, though. Asher stood across from me as I leaned against the wall, and Gin spared a look as I watched. My attention was only on her as she excused herself and let Lydia follow her into the bathroom. I got landed with the kid.

"Some party, right?" Asher nodded down the hall. He wasn't the same annoying little shit he had been when we first got stuck with him. "Hey, you caught the garter. Why aren't you wearing it?" But he was still annoying.

I cocked my eyebrow at him.

He grinned, raising his hands to disregard his own question. "Can't believe Kane and Kit..." Then he was off.

I'd only needed to add a few nods, one or two "yeps" maybe a "no shit?" here and there for the kid to keep talking. He could go on forever if you'd let him. The only space I had in my head was for watching the door and grabbing Gin as soon as she left the bathroom.

"No shit?" I said when Asher looked at me, ignoring his nod as the door opened. I caught Gin when she tried to slip by us. "Catch you later, kid. I gotta have a chat with Gin." I offered Lydia a nod then moved farther down the hall, ignoring the low curses Gin muttered as we came to a darkened room at the end of the hallway.

She didn't fight me. I knew if she wanted to get away from me, she could manage that easy enough. I'd seen her take down a 225-pound rugby player that got a little handsy one night in Tacoma. Coors Light bottle straight to his junk. Gin didn't have a bottle on her, but she grew up in the system. She could handle me well enough if she wanted to get away from me.

"Five. Damn. Minutes," she said when I closed the door behind us, and the overhead motion sensor lit up the dimmers. "I mean it, Hunter. Five."

Shit. She threw my surname at me. My "Motherfucker, I'm gonna cut you" warnings were sounding.

"Fine. I'll get to it," I told her, feeling stupid and twisted up and, yeah, okay, jealous that Carelli had managed to convince her she'd do better away from Seattle, from her friends, from the job she loved, from the home she knew. From me. It hadn't been hard to do. "Gingerb..." I clammed up, taking the glare she gave me as another warning. "You can't go to New York."

Gin blinked, taking a step back like I'd gotten my hands on sensitive information above my security level. Damn that. My paygrade was higher than hers.

"How the hell did you hear about that?"

"I got ears. Besides, that asshole practically announced it not two hours ago." She nodded, stepping away from me with her arms folded, gaze down like she needed to take a second and not look at me. She didn't react when I stepped closer. So close that I caught something that smelled like flowers coming off her neck. It made my mouth water. "You... you can't go," I tried again.

Gin jerked her gaze at me. "Why the hell not?"

The memory was fuzzy. It came back to me in fragmented images, but I remembered kissing Gin that night on Kane and Kiel's balcony. I just couldn't help myself. Gin had stayed with me, keeping watch. We drank coffee spiked with whiskey and watched the perimeter at three in the morning, talking about nothing at all, listening to the forest around us, side by side. There was nothing to say then. Just the sound of our own breathing and the heat between us to keep us company. The day and the whiskey we'd poured into our coffee had gotten to her, and Gin had leaned against me as she started to nod off. I hadn't hated the way it felt, having her light weight against me, feeling the curve of her breast against my arm.

I'd kissed her because it wasn't in me to stop myself. There'd been too much wanting. Too much hoping. Too much wondering and I didn't think. Her eyes had slipped closed, and that beautiful face covered with moonlight made her look fucking sweet and beautiful, and I...just needed to kiss her. Soft, like. Simple. Because I wanted her. Because I suspected she wanted me too.

That night, I took just a little bit of her.

Wanted that again. Right now.

But right here at Kane and Kit's wedding wasn't like the dead silence of the Kaino cabin. Back then, I'd leaned forward, pressed a kiss against her lips. I meant to make it quick just to test the waters. Just to see what it felt like, and when I pulled away from her, Gin's eyes were open, and she reached for me. She held my face still and kissed me back.

From what I could piece together, it had never gone further than that because hell broke loose, and we had to fight. Then Trudy. Then drama. And now here we stood with the distance of a solid year and the distraction of Kiel's asshole brother-in-law and my utter lack of doing a damn thing to give Gin what I suspected she wanted getting in the way.

Now, I couldn't let anything stop me.

"Because...because I..."

"There's nothing, not one damn thing left for me here, Dale." She stood up straight.

My throat felt thick, and my chest twisted again as I watched her. Trudy had wanted everything I was, and

I gave it freely. I thought I'd get the same back from her. I'd taken and given and given more until I could not give her anything else. I'd given to my siblings, and my kid brother had almost gotten me killed for it. Gin? I didn't know if I could risk what losing her again would do to me. The first time had nearly done me in.

"There's something here for you..."

Gin held her breath, clearly waiting. Her hands clenched into fists at her sides as she watched me. But the words got jumbled, felt awkward and stupid the more I thought about them.

"It's just I think there's something..."

Would she stay? For how long? With me? Could I keep her safe? Would I make her happy? Fuck, my head felt too big. My thoughts buzzed around like an overcrowded beehive, a fucking jumble I couldn't get clear of. I couldn't think straight.

Gin's expression fell as she waited.

The seconds I didn't speak up made her mouth dip lower. I panicked, feeling like an asshole even before I spoke. "I mean, Kit needs...well, and the...the show and..."

Gin dropped her shoulders.

I swear I spotted a flush of pink coloring her cheeks, a clear sign that she was pissed. Head shaking, she grunted, "Un-fucking-believable," before she turned and walked toward the door.

I managed to catch her just as she turned the handle.

"No, wait." The door slammed shut when I pressed it, and I left my hand there, palm flat against the frame, right next to her head.

Her lips were full, thick, and drawn back like she was about to scream at me. "Don't you dare think that you can..."

I silenced her with a kiss. Taking her chin in one hand, guiding her head upward to angle her mouth closer. She tasted like cotton candy. Soft and sweet. Her lips warm, growing hotter, and I molded like putty against her, my fingers on her neck, cradling her head.

I saw stars, a long whirl of air whooshing out of me when Gin sucker-punched me right in the gut.

"You son of a bitch!" She shoved me out of her way before she threw the door back and marched down the hallway.

Chapter Six
Gin

A girl could get used to the good life. Well, the good life *and* her own DIY show.

Okay.

The good life, her own show, and a man as hot as Johnny Carelli looking at her the way he looked at me.

Lord.

"I like that smile, *bella*." He worked his gaze across my face and over my body.

Johnny Carelli was a dangerous man, especially when he looked at you the way he looked at me now.

"How can you tell when you're eyeballing my boobs?"

"Skills." He walked toward me, passing Angelo, his assistant, a black folder that he didn't look at. "Practiced, honed skills." Johnny touched my shoulders, moving his fingers down my biceps to grab my hands. He looked to his right, lifting his chin when the director cleared his throat. *"Perfetto."*

I liked the way he held on to me. I shouldn't have. This was all new, weird, and unlike anything else I'd ever experienced. Never had anyone taken the reins from me like Johnny, and I hadn't decided if I liked it. Cara had reintroduced Johnny and me after I'd left the cabin when her brother had stuck around Seattle to make sure his little sister was safe. He'd spotted the tension between Dale and me, and I guess Johnny figured it would be fun to see if he could wrangle a laugh from me.

He had. Three weeks after the shootout. Three weeks after I'd vacated Kiel and Kane's cabin for the quiet seclusion of my own rental near the city.

Johnny had brought me two more bottles of his father's Barolo, and we drank it together. Right out on my front porch swing with his long, muscular arm stretched out behind my shoulder and Otis Redding pumping from my vintage record player. The only pause in our conversation came when "I've Been Loving You Too Long" came on, and a flood of memory engulfed me.

Johnny must have sensed that the song was tied up in whatever he thought was going on with Dale and me. He left the swing, casually replacing Otis with Frank Sinatra's "Something Stupid," from the stack of records I'd forgotten I had in the back.

"Better," he told me, returning to the swing. "Not a person alive who can listen to Frank and not be in a good mood." Then he refilled my glass and spent the rest of the night making me laugh until my stomach hurt. He didn't push but he did stick around, and that pissed Dale off, which made me happy.

It kind of became a routine.

The man in question squeezed my fingers, offering me a smile that made his sharp, angular features more defined. More impossibly handsome. "David will give you your cues, and the lines will be right in the teleprompter. You've rehearsed it. You're fucking beautiful. You're a natural."

"Bet you say that to all the redheads you meet."

"Just the ones with asses like yours, *bella*."

I paused, a little caught up in his teasing honesty and the grin he gave me as I stood on my mark and let the makeup woman fiddle with my hair. "You know, some part of my brain is shouting that I should be offended by that comment," I told him, ignoring how devilishly handsome that man looked when he smiled at me.

"That comes from years of independent thinking telling you every man has an angle." He handed Angelo the phone he'd been messing with to give me his full attention.

"That independent thinking has served me well for a long time." I adjusted my collar, not bothered by Johnny's widening grin. "Besides, I know dang well you've got an angle."

"Of course I do, *cara*. I'm a man with a pulse. I've been angling my way toward you for a year." When I threw him a glare, Johnny amended. "I'm teasing you. This," he said, waving around the set, motioning to the loft rooftop the crew had outfitted with the makings of what would be an urban oasis, "this is all business. Promise."

He *promised* that wasn't what he was doing when he found me in Portland. The visits to Seattle were one thing. The spontaneous trips to Portland when the network agreed to my request for a reassignment were something else. He'd been teasing me with an offer for my own show. A pet project he swore would be all mine with no strings attached.

Johnny *promised* treating me to clothes and a new haircut in an exclusive Portland salon was just his way of being friendly.

He *promised* that a little shopping trip to a few designer boutiques was his way of extending that friendliness. Didn't matter that I kept refusing his gifts and his kindness.

The man was persistent.

Hell, Johnny had even *promised* being my date to Kane and Kit's wedding was just to keep me company. Not to do more sweet-talking about getting me to leave my gig at the network and come to New York with him.

Then, Dale happened.

Dale was always happening.

One look at him, one five-minute conversation had decided for me.

Years at Dale's side had taught me a lot. Like how to bury feelings and desire way down deep where not even I would recognize what I felt.

At first, I couldn't entertain anything more than friendship. He'd been married. He'd loved Trudy, and then Dale didn't love anyone or anything but the liquor he tore through and the job we did day in and out.

He only loved the misery he was in, and that I buried even deeper because I couldn't let him wallow in it all on his own. Even with his complaining, I helped him. Tried to, at least. I told Dale I had his back, told myself it was because he needed it.

The truth was, the things I buried didn't stay underground long. They came up easy, between the nights he lay passed out slurring on my sofa, pretending he felt no pain for the losses in his life, pretending it was only hatred he'd ever let himself feel anymore for anyone. Pretending he didn't see how I looked at him. I hadn't figured out why I took care of him the way I had for so long. Pretending he'd never touched me.

I just couldn't do it anymore.

I took Johnny's job to put distance between Dale and me.

Had to do it, for my own sanity.

"We ready?" the director asked, voice a little low, as though he weren't yet sure how much control he had on this set. The man's attention shifted between Johnny's broad grin and my cocked eyebrow.

"We're ready," I answered, shaking my head to get myself back in the game and the first shoot. "I'm... good to go."

"Excellent." The man motioned toward the cameraman.

I blocked out the flirting smile on Johnny's face and the crew that surrounded us. I knew they likely thought I was a hack—the amateur best friend of the real pro. Kit was the talent. I was just her backup. It was likely I'd fall flat on my face, no matter how many times Johnny tried to convince me I was perfect for the vision he had.

The attention in the room centered on me—a small congregation of strangers who could likely read how scared I was, how green. But I inhaled, remembering that this was my chance. This was my moment to have a say. Another one might not come my way. Just then, there were no judgments, no flirting mafia princes angling for anything. There were no gruff former SEALs incapable of loving me back. Then, there was only me and the moment I had every intention of taking.

"Hi, y'all, I'm Gin Sullivan and this—" I waved around the beginnings of our humble work site "—is Urban Homestead."

"Perfect. Did I say that?"

"About twenty times."

"Well, shit. It was. *Man,* that was perfect." David waved a glass in my direction, leaning against Johnny's desk like he didn't need or want an invitation. "I mean...wow."

I wasn't sure what to make of the director's appraisal of me. It was half amazed astonishment and half close judgment, like he wasn't exactly sure the shoot we'd just completed had gone as smoothly as he'd thought.

"I mean, sincerely, *honestly,* that could not have been better." He moved closer, seeming to forget for a second that Johnny sat between us on the other side of the massive wooden desk. His large frame like a statue David knew was there but was too distracted to remember. As though something loomed just over his shoulder waiting to pounce. Some anxious pigeon ready to peck out the man's eyes if he moved any closer to me.

But then, that might be my imagination or the effects of the three glasses of champagne I'd already downed at this informal post-shoot party inside Johnny's small set office.

"I got a feeling." I smiled behind my drink, arms crossed as he wiggled closer. "It felt...good, you know?" The question was rhetorical. Meant more for myself, but I heard Johnny's small laugh behind me and spotted David's slow nod. Both reminded me that I had an audience—two men with an interest in me for very different and likely very similar reasons.

"It *was* good. It was more than..."

"What did I tell you?" Johnny slapped David on the back as he stood.

The director's surprise caught me off guard, as though the quick movement from his boss and the loudness of his voice reminded everyone why we were there and who was in charge.

Johnny came around the desk and took David's glass from him, placing it at the man's side. The party ended with no more than Johnny's warm but final smile that ushered the director away from me.

I had a smile on my face, and my head felt fuzzy. Champagne filled me up almost as much as the adrenaline buzz that kept me grinning.

Johnny turned from the door, those beautifully broad shoulders against the wall behind him, and even the small intoxication I felt seemed to dim.

Still, he went silent. That ever-present grin proud and satisfied, so much so that it made me pause. I blinked at him, forgetting the thoughts that kept me from relishing the thrill of the moment.

"What?" I put down my glass, ignoring my cell when it chimed with a text alert. "What's the grin about?"

"You." He pushed off the wall, coming to stand directly in front of me. "I had you pegged the second I walked into Kaino's cabin. Spitfire redhead mad at that dumb redneck." When I frowned, not appreciating the reminder of how mad Dale had made me that night, Johnny seemed to catch on quick and hurried to kill the distance between us with his massive palms at my sides on his desk. He smelled faintly of cigar smoke and brandy. I caught the delicious hint of peppermint on his breath when he exhaled, gaze working over my face like he couldn't quite believe what he saw when he watched me.

A man like Johnny Carelli was intimidating. He was handsome and strong. The sort of man who had a presence. One that lingered when he entered a room and made his way around it. He caught attention and kept it like it belonged to him, and he dared anyone to argue with him about the possession. That kind of presence would humble even the strongest. But there wasn't a person alive who could accuse Johnny of being cruel or rude when he wanted on your good side, and Johnny had *always* wanted on my good side.

But I wasn't some simple woman right off the turnip truck. I had a brain, and my hearing was excellent. Kiel had warned me, so had Cara. The Carellis weren't a simple philanthropic family. They weren't humble businesspeople. They were criminals. They had ties I probably didn't want to know about. Ties Cara told me never to ask her brother about. I trusted her, even if I didn't trust him.

Johnny was intimidating and handsome. He stood less than three feet from me, his mouth very close to mine. He'd been closer before, but he'd never kissed me, not really. A peck on the cheek or a hug that lingered, but he'd never pushed like I'd always expected him to. There was something that held him back which he didn't seem eager to talk about. But then, I hadn't exactly been ready to take what was happening between us anywhere beyond a business arrangement. But now, with him looking the way he was, I wondered if Johnny would ask me to.

"And...um, what did you think about the spitfire?" I asked when he went on looking me over, because the way he watched me became too much for me. "Other than all the cursing you heard me doing."

"I thought—" he moved closer, fingertips teasing against my cheek "—that whoever hurt you that badly, had you that mad, was the stupidest asshole in the world." He brought his gaze to my mouth.

I stopped breathing.

"Having met that particular asshole, I can say I wasn't so wrong."

Dale's face flashed into my mind. Damn it all to hell. Just the mention of him could ruin a moment I might want. Or might not want. Lord, I wish I knew which it was.

Johnny seemed to notice the distraction that had me looking away. He exhaled, releasing my face. I couldn't decide if I hated how cold my skin felt without him touching me there or if I was relieved he wasn't going to kiss me.

"I ruin our little moment?" He stepped back.

I was saved from answering when my phone chimed with another alert. I ignored it, deciding my new boss deserved my full attention.

Johnny cocked an eyebrow, as though he were surprised.

My smile came easy. Something that seemed to make his tight features relax. "I might be one of those rare animals that isn't compelled to look at my phone whenever it moves or chirps or chimes for attention."

He sat next to me, sliding my cell over to make room for himself. "Aren't you on the endangered species list?"

I nodded, sighing dramatically because I liked when I could make Johnny Carelli, that imposing, intimidating man, laugh.

He did just then, and I liked the sound of it. "They say repopulation is the best way to get off that list."

It was my turn to laugh. The noise that left my mouth fell somewhere between a shocked gasp and a soft snort of surprise. He always seemed able to one-up me with sarcastic responses, a lost art we both were practiced in.

"Well, I think you'd have to give me a heck of a lot more than my own show, Mr. Carelli, if you want that to happen."

Another chirp sounded, and I leaned toward my phone, glancing at the screen before I shrugged, smiling back at Johnny. "Kit wants to know how today went."

"She's your friend. You should tell her."

"I meant to call her *and* your sister."

"*I* told my sister."

Johnny ignored me when I tilted my head at him, wondering why he'd reported back to Cara before I had a chance to. "You did?"

He nodded, glancing down at me, stretching his feet out in front of his desk. "My sister is a control freak, especially when it comes to her friends. Or me."

"Or you and her friends?"

He laughed again. There was a light in his dark eyes that had something warm creeping into my chest. "*Si,* especially with me and her friends. *Oddio,* she thinks I'm going to do...dishonorable things to you..."

"Well..."

He glanced my way, flashing his attention to me. The grin he tried to keep off his mouth told me Johnny wasn't angry. "You're as bratty as she is." When I narrowed my eyes at him, Johnny shook his head, not able to back that one up. "Okay, no one is as bratty as Cara."

"No, I don't think anyone is. But I'm glad you spoke to her." Another alert and I picked up my phone, holding it between my fingers to keep my hands occupied.

Johnny moved closer, and I caught another whiff of a scent, this one reminding me of rich, expensive cologne.

I moved my nails across the back of my phone, letting the noise of the tapping distract me. "Between the prep work before the shoot, the shoot itself, and the little after party, I didn't have time to call Kit or Cara and tell them anything."

Yet again, my phone sounded, and this time, Johnny pulled my phone from my hands, sliding his thumb across the screen before I could protest.

"Listen, Mrs. Kaino..." His demeanor changed in an instant. The wide, warm smile vanished from Johnny's face. "*Si*," he said, standing from the desk. He moved around the room, his shoulders and back going straight, and the muscles in his neck flexed as Johnny turned. He slipped one hand into his pocket as he listened to whoever it was spoke to him on my phone. "No. That's not going to happen. No."

He faced the window, ignoring me when I left the desk, following behind him. I wanted to interrupt. To demand that he give me back my phone, but Johnny had shifted from calm and collected to outright pissed off in the few seconds since he'd answered that call. He'd always wanted on my good side. I'd never seen anything else from him. But the person on the other end of the call wasn't anyone Johnny Carelli had any interest in a good side connections with.

He tightened his features. I watched his profile, not liking how he flared his nostrils or how he sucked on the inside of his cheek. The longer the person spoke, the more irritated Johnny became.

"Johnny...what on earth..."

He flashed me a glare. In an instant, the hard edges that made his expression seem so dangerous, so scary, softened.

"That all you have to say? *Bene*."

Then Johnny hung up the phone. He held it for half a second, pressing his lips together, attention on the cityscape outside the window before he handed my cell back to me.

"I'm sorry, *bella*," he told me, smoothing his fingers across my forehead to brush back my bangs. "But I think I pissed off your asshole redneck."

Chapter Seven
Dale

Gin was different now.

Maybe it was the city.

It had done something to her.

Only a week in New York and she'd started to wear her surroundings like a second skin. Maybe it was just how she stood. There were heels now, not wellies or Chucks like the ones she'd sported on the set back in Seattle.

I watched her like a damn stalker from a bus stop across four lanes of traffic on one of the busiest streets in Manhattan, wondering how in the hell I'd managed to go years, damn years, not noticing Gin's legs.

I was a blind asshole.

Had to be the heels.

Or the city.

Back in Washington, she was all business, calling the T-shirts and a worn pair of Levi's her behind-the-scenes-shit. Clothes that made her presentable enough to work hard but not look like a truck driver.

There was still a fit shape to her. No number of baggy tees, messy ponytails, and rubber boots could hide that. But I'd somehow missed some very important details, like those legs.

Watching her as she talked with some chick, I noticed Gin was different in more ways than I'd picked up on at the wedding. Now there was something about her that made me feel...out of place. She looked like a lady. I was damn sure no gentleman. How she'd changed, what she'd become, all that might have been there all along, but I'd missed it.

I'd missed a lot of things.

I was here to stop missing everything.

"This is not a good idea," Kane had warned yesterday before I caught my flight. He'd followed me around the Tacoma set like a kid trying to get his old man not to take off on yet another bender. He was my boss, my friend, but the bastard wasn't my keeper. "Seriously, dude..."

"Shouldn't you be on your honeymoon?"

"Shouldn't you be leaving well enough alone?"

Asshole had to say shit like that. I understood. Kit had his ear, and Gin had Kit's. After that conversation with Carelli, my gut screamed at me to carry my ass to New York.

"Remind Bowtie these are a loan. I'm coming back for them." I stuffed my drills and bits into Asher's truck bed and covered them with a tarp. "I'm serious. Do not let that little asshole mess up my shit."

"Dale..." Kane watched me across the truck.

I could feel his stare, the weight of it like a noose around my neck. I looked around the set, to the crew. Kit stood at the edge of the mansion, pretending to listen to one of the assistant producers. She watched Kane and me closer, likely trying to read our lips.

They were good people.

They cared about Gin.

Hell, I knew they cared about me too.

Head down, staring at the rust spotted around Asher's truck bed, I shook my head. "He's in the fucking mob." I finally looked up at him. "From the shit he said to me, I got the feeling he's not letting her go easy, and I'm not going to leave her up there with no one having her back."

"Man," he started, clenching his teeth as if he questioned the wisdom of telling me what he thought. The next second, though, Kane exhaled and got out what was in his head. "She's managed a year on her own. Gin is a baller. She's a badass. You should know better than anyone she can cover her own ass." He wasn't wrong, but I didn't have time to discuss it. There was a plane to catch and a plan in play. Or at least, part of one—get to New York.

"It's your funeral," Kane told me, not smiling. "Just remember I warned you."

Kane didn't get it. No one would, I guess, unless they'd been where I had. There was civilian loyalty, and there was service loyalty. You didn't know what it was until you'd seen action. I had. Kane hadn't, and even though Gin hadn't been in the service, she'd done time being loyal. She'd had a shitty childhood. She'd spent time in the foster system. She'd had to learn what real loyalty was. When your back was against the wall, there weren't many you could count on. Gin had proven to me time and again I could count on her.

Sometimes, she was the only one I could count on.

The traffic thickened as Gin and her friend went on talking until the woman with the portfolio got into the limo and Gin waved her off. She watched the car drive away, and I moved closer, slipping through the throng of cars.

Gin pulled out her phone, speaking to the porter at the hotel entrance. The guy hailed a cab as Gin's attention was on that phone.

My stomach coiled, realizing her guard was down, willing her with my stare to put the damn cell away as a group of kids came near her.

Two of them veered away from the small group, shooting glances at Gin, then to each other. They couldn't have been more than eighteen, thin, wearing thick coats and caps pulled down to their eyebrows. There were pale with pimpled skin, and the lankiest of the two rushed right behind Gin before I'd cleared a row of speeding cabs.

The kid went for her purse, yanking it from her shoulder. Gin jumped, surprised by the tussle, but quickly recovered. She shook her head once before she took the heel of her shoe and slammed it into the top of the kid's foot, sending the little punk to his side.

"Are you freaking crazy, you little bastard?" she yelled, hovering over him, pointing at him, and continuing to jab her heel into the top of his foot.

The porter and two of the hotel bellhops had to pull Gin off the kid before a cruiser approached. The entire time, she screamed bloody murder at this wailing, lanky kid who babbled and cried over his busted foot.

"Idiot," I mumbled, calling out the kid for what he was and myself for thinking Gin would need a rescue. Of course, this was a stupid attempt by a little punk with no clue. New York was big, and Carelli wasn't exactly a Boy Scout. I wasn't simple.

Gin could be in a lot of trouble if she stayed around him for too long, but I hated to admit it. Kane wasn't totally wrong. She wasn't helpless, a fact that I should have remembered. God knows I'd seen her handle herself one time too many.

Like the first night I met her.

The night Kit had planned to interview Gin for her job.

Kit had laughed louder than I'd ever seen her that night. We stayed in the corner away from the noise in the bar as Kane and I each nursed a beer. Back then, the bastard liked to pretend he wasn't stupid over

Kit. He played bodyguard to protect the network's investment and any future livelihood the show might have for him, but I knew better. The guy was sprung for Kit even then.

I'd only made out Kit's laugh and the back of Gin's head as they sat and talked for hours on end. I was about to check out and leave Kane to his bodyguarding when Kit's laughing stopped altogether.

"What the hell did you say to us?" Kit's voice went louder than the music blaring from the speakers at the back of the bar.

Even with the crowd, Kane and I both heard the whip of insult and anger in her voice.

"Shit," Kane had said, kicking off the barstool at the same time I did.

We made it near Kit's table just as Kit and Gin stood, and some fat cowboy took hold of Kit's arm.

"I said, no thank you." Kit and Gin stood shoulder to shoulder.

I took half a second to assess the situation—fat cowboy who looked to be pushing fifty and hardly able to stand, and Kit's potential employee, a curvy woman with a hurricane of dark red hair, looking at the drunk asshole like she was ready to rip him from neck to nuts.

The asshole was too drunk to notice his request and presence weren't wanted, and he angled closer to Kit, getting out a sloppy, "Come on, darlin', one dance..."

Kane glanced at me and nodded toward the back of the bar. I slipped over the counter as he bypassed the stage. But just as we made it to the table, Kit had maneuvered out of the fat asshole's grip and Gin had swiped his legs out from under him.

Problem was, the cowboy had two drunk friends who looked eager for a fight, and when he went down and they spotted the two small women responsible, they charged, not expecting either Kit or Gin to do much damage.

Idiots, the pair of them.

Gin was on a second cowboy's back, her legs around his waist, holding her arm around his neck as he swung back and forth, struggling to shake her loose.

I was impressed.

She looked like a force of nature. It didn't occur to me that she needed me for a single thing. So I just stood there, grinning like a fool because she was something else to look at.

Hell, she had such a lock on the guy's neck, that asshole's face was turning purple.

"Hand that over," she said, surprising me with the demand.

Next to me on a stand-up speaker sat a warm bottle of Teeling Irish Whiskey, the label peeled at the corner, and Gin kept nodding to it. For some reason, the sight of this woman looking half crazed with violence put me in a good mood, kind of made me miss my SEAL brothers.

I grinned at her, forgetting for a second that Trudy was going to bitch at me if I came home with a busted lip for getting in the middle of someone else's tussle. But, hell, it looked like fun.

"Well?" she grunted, squeezing the asshole's neck tighter when I didn't answer.

"Half full," I said, expecting her to understand. "Seems a shame to waste."

Behind us, Kane knocked out the drunk asshole who'd insisted Kit dance with him and managed, somehow, to hold her and the asshole's friend back. Gin dropped the second guy to the floor, kneeing him for good measure, then jerked the Teeling from the speaker, twisted the cap open, threw back the bottle, and downed the whiskey.

"Now it's not," she said, flipping it upside down. The guy rolled over and came back for her, and then Gin knocked him good across the back of the head.

I hadn't seen anyone move that quickly, or down liquor like that, since I left the SEALs. Right then, I knew if Kit didn't hire Gin, I'd find a way to get her on our crew. This woman was a badass. You could never have too many of those in your life.

I glanced at the three men on the floor, then at Kit and Kane before offering Gin my hand. "Dale Hunter," I said, nodding as she shook it. "You taking the job?"

"Yeah," Gin answered, shrugging like she didn't see any reason not to. "Might as well."

"Good. Let me buy you a drink."

Gin disappeared inside the hotel with the porter and two bellhops following behind her. She looked like a queen, angry and ready to burn the fucking city to the ground because some punk kid tried to swipe her purse.

I was a moron.

Of course, she could handle herself.

Of course, she could manage a kid and a city. Probably an entire army of dangerous men.

Of course, she'd get tired of me running from the shit that'd weighed me down my whole life.

Gin was dangerous herself. She was beautiful, smart, and talented.

Of course, someone like Carelli would see that.

Who wouldn't?

Somewhere inside the bullshit I'd locked away in my head, there was a voice that reminded me what I wanted and how to get it. I knew what I wanted. I just had to convince Gin that I meant it. I had to convince her to give me a chance to prove to her that it wasn't too late.

My cell vibrated in my pocket, and I pulled it out, eyes rolling when I spotted Kiel's name on the screen. I only answered because he was my in on Carelli. Those people might be his in-laws, but Kiel owed me. I had a bullet hole in my gut because of that asshole. No way was he ever gonna repay that shit.

"Yeah?"

"Sunshine! Good to see New York has improved your attitude." The low grunt I made seemed answer enough for Kiel, and the man continued. "Fine, I won't mess with you. My beautiful wife is about to pop, and my son could come at any second, so I'm in a rush and feeling fucking generous." Another grunt and this time, Kiel went silent.

"Three-hour surgery, asshole."

He sighed, clearing his throat before he continued. "Fine, okay. So, my big brother says you have no plan."

"I'm not an idiot."

"You let that beautiful woman fall right into my brother-in-law's rich, capable hands, Hunter. You being an idiot is a given, but I digress." In the background, I caught Cara's soft, singsong voice, and Kiel's attitude instantly changed. "Yes, baby. I know." He cleared his throat, getting rid of any sweetness he reserved for his wife before he spoke to me again. "Okay, man, I got an idea. It's a good one."

For a second, I remembered Kiel's grumpy complaining at the party and how irritated he'd been at his brother-in-law. Turned out Kiel needed to learn not to go into a poker game buzzed. He'd complained about the money Carelli had won off of him for the rest of the weekend. The bastard had his pride, and I suspected whatever had him calling was likely tied up in the money Johnny Carelli took from him in that game.

"This have anything to do with that ten grand you lost?"

"You know it does." He didn't sound remotely embarrassed, and Kiel didn't miss a beat when he hurried to ask, "You got cash on you?"

"I do."

"Good. Grab an Uber. I'll text you an address. There's someone you should meet."

The text alert sounded on my phone, and I looked at it. The hair on my arms stood up. That was never good. I caught the same vibe on assignment when shit was about to get squirrelly. Sometimes, it meant that we'd come across the mark we'd been tagged with finding. Sometimes, it meant we'd been made, and some asshole was waiting to detonate a bomb and blow us to pieces out into the desert.

But this? Hell, it could go either way.

"So," I asked Kiel, jaw clenching as I readied for what I was sure would be a smartass response. "Is this gonna earn me a pair of cement boots?"

He laughed, and the sound did not make me feel any better. "No, but my brother-in-law probably won't be extending any more poker invites to me."

Chapter Eight

Gin

Back in East Tennessee, we got swarms. Heat came in swarms, same as the dust that coated the mountains and the pollen that dried around the rivers. Everything stuck, and even breathing got tricky for some.

Old Lady Mixen, the last foster mother I had, used to say that was why God made Tennessee so pretty—so we'd forget the way allergy season made even shallow breaths a burden.

We had other swarms too, like the fireflies that came into the mountains in mid-June. Those, I welcomed because they were beautiful. Great heaps of light moving together like choreographed swirls, brightening the dark sky, whisking around this way and that. There was nothing in my world more beautiful than those creatures dancing.

Some swarms were beautiful, even welcome.

But the swarm of heat I felt standing on the job site Monday morning was overbearing. I'd only felt it before when Dale stared too long. When he stared and said nothing. When he stared, said nothing, and dangled that pointless hope in front of me.

Like he did then, walking straight for me.

"Son of a bitch," I whispered behind my cup as I widened my eyes, blinking to test if I was imagining the man coming straight for me.

Johnny's gaze left my face, shifted across the roof. He stood straight up, handing over his coffee to Angelo in front of me and trying to keep Dale from getting a good look at me.

Something, I hated to admit, I didn't appreciate.

Dale wore what I loved seeing him in—a pair of well-worn Levi's, combat boots, a tight gray Navy shirt, with a thin, dark blue flannel unbuttoned and rolled up to his elbows. He looked tired, rugged, and I had to fight back the low rush of desire that swirled in the pit of my stomach when I spotted him coming closer. He wore no hat but had on a pair of black shades that concealed half of his face. The other half was covered in a scruffy beard that looked heavier than how he'd worn it at Kit and Kane's wedding.

"You lost, Hunter?" Johnny held up a hand when Dale tilted his head.

Dale's gaze shot over Johnny's shoulder to look right at me. He didn't answer. Instead, Dale shifted the corner of his mouth, and his expression cleared as he watched me. He had nothing to say to Johnny—that look alone told me as much.

"Why are you here?" I asked him, sidestepping my boss.

I didn't need a bodyguard, not from Dale. *Especially* not from Dale. When the man only watched me, the scrutiny too quiet, too focused for my liking, I looked away, nodding at the crew. "We've got a long day ahead of us and no time for drama."

"I'm here to work." His voice was low, a deep, gravelly tone as though he'd either just finished an all-night drunk or hadn't yet shaken off his sleep.

"We got a full crew." Johnny looked back at me, not waiting for my confirmation before he glared back at Dale. "You can go." Then he poked Dale's shoulder once.

I groaned, knowing if I didn't defuse the situation before it started, things would get messy.

Dale looked down once, right at the spot where Johnny had touched him, glanced up, jaw tightening, nostrils flaring, though he didn't utter a sound. But I noticed the way he worked his throat. How he swallowed once. How he curled one fist at his side. How the knuckles there grew white.

I immediately stood in front of him, shaking off Johnny's hand when he tried pulling me back. "Give me a minute." I didn't bother to look at Johnny.

"Bella..."

"Johnny, please."

He backed away but didn't leave us space enough for any real privacy. That didn't bother me as much as Dale just showing up on my set, no matter how damn good he looked.

"Why am I always repeating myself with you?" I didn't expect him to answer. I waved him off when he opened his mouth, and I held up my phone. "I'm giving you five minutes," I said, just like I had the night of Kit and Kane's wedding. I slid a thumb across the screen until I found the clock app and set the timer to five, showing him the screen when I hit the "Start" button. "Explain yourself."

"Don't need five," he said. To demonstrate his confidence, Dale took off his shades, tucking them into the neck of his shirt, seeming to want a better look at me.

I wished he hadn't. One look at his eyes told me he hadn't had an all-night drunk. He was tired. I'd know that look anywhere. The man wasn't sleeping, probably hadn't been for a while.

As quickly as the worry inched into my head, I pushed it down. I reminded myself that I was supposed to be in the city forgetting this man. Forgetting everything that was and would never be between us.

"Four and a half."

"You look good."

I shook my head, letting my temper cradle me, heat me up from the inside.

Dale's mouth twitched. He shot a glance at Johnny but didn't seem too concerned by the way the other man cleared his throat or how he'd moved half a step closer. "Gotta say, that was a hell of a gut punch you landed back at the reception."

"Okay, now it's three minutes." I waved my phone at him, emphasizing my point. I didn't need a reminder of the out-of-nowhere kiss Dale had planted on me or how pissed off it had made me. I hoped that jab to his gut had burned like fire. "Why the hell are you here?"

Dale exhaled, digging into his back pocket to produce a slip of paper. "Told you. I'm here to work."

"You don't work for me."

"No, I don't." Dale waved the paper at Johnny but kept his attention on me. "I work for Carelli Enterprises. Hired last night, in fact. Nice meeting I had with Mr. Carelli."

"Figlio di puttana!" Johnny cursed, grabbing the paper from Dale. He tore through it, reading the letter before I could make out more than the Carelli letterhead on the top of the page. "You have some brass fucking balls," he told Dale, standing inches from him. Angelo held Johnny back.

I grabbed Dale's arm, though it wasn't necessary. The SEAL didn't move, did little more than watch Johnny, his expression unimpressed, a little bored as my boss glared at him.

To the director, David, Johnny snapped, "Take an hour, get the crew sorted. I'm going to have a conversation with my father," before he and Angelo left.

Dale watched them leave, a grin pulling at the corners of his mouth.

"He's not happy."

"He's not the only dang one." I pulled Dale's attention away from Johnny and down at me. The half smile fell from his face.

"Listen...Gin..." He at least had sense enough to look ashamed.

"You can save it." I waved off any explanation he might have had. I headed back into the apartment and away from my former best friend. The skeleton crew focused on the work outside since there would be no rain today and the temperatures would be mild. I'd set up a small design studio in what would be the dining room while Jess, the designer I'd hired to help focus my ideas, came up with sketches, finalized the plans for the next few weeks' shoots. That was where I intended to hide from Dale, hoping he'd get the hint and leave me alone.

He knew my temper.

He knew when I needed my space, but it seemed a year apart had done something to Dale and his memory of what I needed and when I needed those things.

The bastard followed right behind me. "I didn't traipse halfway across the damn country to see you just so you could tell me to fuck off and hide out in..."

"Fuck off." I threw a middle finger over my shoulder as I bypassed one of the producers in the living room.

"That any way to talk to one of your crew?" He sounded like an asshole with that small, teasing laugh in his tone.

I stopped near the kitchen to turn and glare at him. "You are not, not, *not* a member of this crew."

"Carelli's daddy seems to think I am."

"What did you do?" I watched him.

Dale wasn't friendly. He didn't get along with other people. He wasn't all that charming.

So how the hell did he manage to slink his way on to Johnny's pet project without anyone knowing?

I hated how handsome he was. Hated more that he likely knew just how damn handsome he was. He was likely betting that I was still attracted to him to get on my good side. But I didn't think I had a good side anymore.

My good side probably died a good year ago.

"What?" He moved close, stretching a hand to brush back the bangs from my eyes.

"Oh my God," I said, the realization coming to me suddenly. I swatted at his touch. "You got Kiel to talk to his father-in-law."

The asshole shrugged with a cocky grin. "I took a bullet for him."

"Son of a bitch."

"In fact, Gingerbread...""Do *not* call me that."

He didn't pause but twisted his mouth to press his lips together before he spoke. "Took a bullet for you, too."

"That's not saying much. You'd take a bullet for anyone," I told him, ignoring the small grunt in his voice I knew was forced.

Dale didn't beg. He didn't do sympathy, but if he wanted to get his way, he wasn't past reminding you of favors he'd done for you. Leave it to that asshole to remind me of the night I'd spent a year trying to forget. Still, him taking a bullet didn't carry much weight, and we both knew it. I turned toward him when I reached the dining room table.

His shades were hanging from the collar of his Navy tee as Dale's eyes narrowed for a second like he needed a small pause to squint at me. He gave me a once-over to see if I was messing with him before he shook his head. "Well, that fucking stings."

"Please. It's written into your DNA." I suppressed the small twinge of guilt I felt at insulting him. "It's in the training."

"Three-hour surgery." He looked down for a second before he stared at me again, not the least bit contrary or ashamed that he seemed to be milking the I've-been-shot sob story a full year after it happened.

I matched his pathetic attempt with one of my own. "Two-night bender on my sofa."

Dale went quiet then. He seemed surprised by my dig over the weekend he'd been kicked out of every dive bar in Seattle because Trudy had left him for some asshole. Dale wanted to drink away reality, and I let him finish the job on my sofa.

"Fair enough." His tone held less bite, but I knew he wasn't finished comparing wounds that had been inflicted on him. "But you did leave without saying goodbye." He flattened his mouth into a line, like just the memory of my exit from Seattle was a personal insult despite the fact that we weren't speaking at the time.

When I cocked my eyebrow at him, thinking of the last time I left, after the wedding, Dale's jaw clenched, and the muscles in his neck flexed.

"Twice," he muttered.

I couldn't deny that, much as I wanted to.

"And all I want is a chance to say I'm sorry. I just want a chance to make amends." He didn't ease the tension in his face. He didn't relax at all, so that rugged swagger that always had him looking scary and fierce intensified. It was hard for him to beg. He never did that. "If I'm desperate enough to crawl into bed with a criminal and ask his daddy for a job, don't you think that means I'm desperate to get my best friend to talk to me again?"

He was. Very desperate.

I only wanted one explanation from him.

Just one.

After all this time, the fact that he'd gone all stupid and sweet over his ex-wife didn't bother me so much anymore. I just wanted him to acknowledge what he said to me before he got shot.

I needed to hear the words.

But Dale was a stubborn man.

When he didn't want to do something, he didn't. It seemed to me, for whatever his reasons, things needed to be slow. He couldn't jump in with explanations and promises he might not be ready to make.

I could wait. But I wouldn't wait for long.

"Fine, but not here."

He nodded but didn't smile.

"There's a diner around the corner from my hotel called Dakota's. On West 57th."

He nodded again, and the tightness in his face relaxed, though he didn't smile. Dale never smiled outright.

"And don't think just because I'm agreeing that I'm not pissed you're here or that I won't make you work for a living."

"You ever see me not work hard?"

"Never."

"Then give me a job."

"Joe Gates is up on the roof, laying tar." I smiled, not meaning it in the least when Dale flared his nostrils.

He hated tar work. That much I knew from all the times he'd set Asher on the job when we'd come across a building or two in need of it back in Seattle. Seems things hadn't changed, but Dale didn't seem inclined to complain.

I moved several manila folders around, not looking at Dale when I spoke. "It's dirty, filthy work, but you can do it. I know you can."

"I'll get up there."

He walked away, and I couldn't help but watch him. He had swagger. No doubt about that. And an ass that filled out those Levi's perfectly, but my view got interrupted. I tried to pretend like I hadn't been caught staring when Dale abruptly stopped, glancing over his shoulder at me and called my name just a few feet from the door.

"Hey, Gingerbread? This suits you."

"What does?" I pretended again to be interested in the folder in my hands.

Dale nodded to the apartment, moving his head to the materials and fabric lining the window seat. "All this...you...being the center of attention." He smiled, shooting a wink my way I couldn't pretend not to feel in the pit of my stomach. "It suits you."

Chapter Nine
Dale

Johnny Carelli liked to pretend he ran things. Maybe he did.

But from the meeting I'd had with his father, I understood a little better who was in charge.

The old man was just that, damn old. But when I sat down in front of him, I felt stupid and awkward, explaining that I wanted on Johnny's new crew to get back into Gin's good graces. The old man simply watched me.

No noise. No expression. No emotion.

Just cold, calculating eyes looking right through me as he watched me, getting the measure of me as he thought of things he didn't seem inclined to share.

That shit suited me fine. But it took all my reserves

of willpower not to tell the old bastard to speak up or cut me loose.

Until, finally, he did.

"My son-in-law says you were in the Navy."

"Yes, sir." The "sir" felt like dirt on my tongue. I knew the measure of this old man. I knew who and what he was. I knew the business he was in. Didn't much care to be asking someone like him for favors, but for Gin, I'd do just about anything. "SEALs. Twelve years."

His eyebrows went up then, and that confession got his attention. Turned out Old Man Carelli had been stationed in Vietnam back in '72. He'd seen real action. He'd been on the ground, in foxholes and blazing temperatures, shoulder to shoulder with his brothers, bleeding and half dying alongside them.

Gotta respect that level of service.

He seemed to respect my honesty.

"My son fancies himself a businessman," he'd said, picking a grape from a bowl on the cart next to his chair. "He forgets the business our family has always been in. He forgets it's not for the faint of heart." Carelli leaned forward, his expression serious, cold. "He forgets we cannot bring the innocent into this world, and you, my friend, and your woman are innocent."

That had landed me the gig. I guessed Old Man Carelli didn't buy his son's belief that the show would take off. He didn't believe him when the asshole thought he could take Gin wherever she wanted to go, even if that meant his bed.

Next to me, Joe Gates slopped a last section of the roof with tar, and I finished the front. It was stinky, grimy work, nothing worse than I'd done before. Grunt work, to be sure, but Gin seemed to need her distance.

I spotted her as she moved below us. She pointed to a line of raised vegetable beds on the patio. Carelli stood next to her, hands deep in his pockets as the director, David, I think I heard Joe call him, motioned to the beds.

"What do you make of them?" I asked Joe.

The guy stood next to me, stopping to stretch his back and drop the mop next to the tar bucket. "Who?"

"Carelli and the woman."

"The redhead?"

I nodded.

Joe shrugged, moving his head over the roof ledge to get a better look. "They're not fucking. If they were, that guy would be touching her, stroking her back, or holding on to her waist, doing something to let every other asshole on the crew know she's taken."

My gut turned at just the mention of Gin and Carelli together. At just the idea that Gates had probably put thoughts of Gin naked into his head at all, but I shook off the whip of anger I felt. Wouldn't do me any good to piss anyone off first day on the job. That shit would get me nowhere closer to earning her forgiveness.

The day had been a good five degrees hotter than it should have been, and the black tar reflecting the sun made it a hundred times worse. Joe had four empty bottles of water lying next to him. He was tall and had a good fifteen years on me, with brown skin and thin hair. He sat on the roof edge, wiping his face with a damp red bandana, pulling on a half-empty bottle of water as I offered him what I had left in my thermos. Least I could do was share what I had. My thermos was cold, still sweating. I'd bet it was more satisfying than what he'd been sipping on for the past half hour.

"You been on the crew this whole time?"

"Why you asking?" He eyed me like he wanted to know my angle before he answered me or took the water I offered.

"I got my reasons." I grabbed his empty bottle when he dropped it. He watched me closely as I filled it from my thermos, like he wasn't sure what I was playing at, giving him most of my cold water.

Down below, Gin turned away from David, looking up at Carelli as he spoke to her. I caught her profile— still fucking beautiful. Perfect. Out of reach.

I blinked, the vibration of my cell pulling my attention away from Gin as I dug in my pocket to silence the call.

"All I know is Carelli is the money guy and spares no expense." Joe finally took the water I offered him. "Whatever she wants, we get. That was the rule from jump. She wants marble, we get marble. She wants cedar for the raised beds, we get cedar and not treated pine. She wants organic plants, we get organic. Either that asshole wants to impress some studio with high-dollar shit, or he wants to fuck her." He stood, and I rubbed my eyes to distract myself from the truth Joe spoke and I already knew. He stood next to me stretching again as he looked down at the crew below. "I ain't never seen no man spend this much cash on pussy he ain't had." When I jerked my gaze to him, Joe lifted his hand, his gapped-tooth grin white and wide like he'd guessed why I'd asked about Gin and Carelli and my reaction had confirmed it. I'd been caught and didn't bother making an excuse. "Hell, man, it's clear enough. The way you act around her, the way you look at her, the way she looks back at you, I'd swear you'd had her before."

"Get the fuck out of here." I knocked off the man's hand when he slapped my shoulder, ignoring how loud he laughed at me when I shot him the bird.

"I just call 'em like I see 'em."

Joe's laugh carried behind him as he walked toward the exit. I went on ignoring him. He didn't know what he was talking about. I wouldn't be likely to forget ever being with Gin. That was just not something that slipped a man's memory. Not with a woman like Gin.

She was remarkable. I'd always known that. Everyone had. There were things about her I'd noticed even when I shouldn't have. Even when I'd belonged to someone else.

Like that night back in Tacoma, just a few weeks before Trudy left me. Gin had her accusations. Truth was, I had my own suspicions, but I wouldn't let my mind go that way.

It had been our first real fight.

Two weeks later, I'd crawled back to her. I'd begged her to forgive me because she was my only real friend in the world, but the bullshit had started at Lucky's with her warning me of things she'd seen.

Gin had motioned the bartender for another shot of Jack. When the man finished pouring our glasses, she grabbed the neck of the bottle, throwing her Visa on the bar. "Leave it."

"Hell," I'd whispered, tugging off my jacket to lean against the bar.

She'd asked to meet me as we'd left the set, something Gin never did. She had a routine, and Tuesday nights and Lucky's weren't part of it. Tuesday nights usually meant she'd be with her neighbor Madison at some kickboxing class downtown.

Not here on this side of the city.

Not drinking Jack straight from the bottle.

We downed two shots between us before she seemed ready to speak. By the time that happened, her face had gone pink in the cheeks, and her wide eyes glistened like wet glass. She wasn't drunk. I'd seen how much Jack it took to get this woman sauced, and two shots wouldn't come close to it. But Gin seemed determined and, yeah, maybe a little anxious.

"Thing is," she finally said, rolling the empty shot glass between her fingers, attention on the bar as she spoke. *Then the redhead inhaled, blowing out a breath as she looked over at me. "You and me, we're good. Friendly. I like that. I can say stuff to you, and I know you won't laugh at me."*

"'Course not." It was true, but she didn't need me trying to convince her of that fact.

"You don't bullshit with me and, again, I like that. I like people who are honest." She sat up, abandoning the glass to swing her legs around, resting on her elbow. *"I don't think it would be a stretch to say we're friends. Maybe even good friends."*

"I don't disagree with that, Gingerbread."

Her mouth lifted up at the corner, and her body relaxed. *"Good...that's... I'm glad you think that way."*

When she directed her gaze back down to the bottle on the bar and reached for it, I caught the shake in her fingers. How that tremble made her grip on the Jack unsteady, and I took it from her. *"Why don't you relax and tell me what's got you fussed?"*

She watched the whiskey as I filled each of our glasses, and then her eyes were on me.

I felt the shift of tension, how she looked over my profile. Hard to miss when a woman like Gin looked at you that way. Hard to miss it, no matter who you are. She knew I was married. She knew I didn't run around on my woman. Ever.

And she wasn't the sort to try to tempt a man from what he had. She never flirted. She never looked *long at me with any real intention. If she did, those looks got lost behind blinks or jokes or things she'd never take further.*

But there was something in the way she said my name. In the things she did for me. How she listened, really listened, something I'd never felt with any of my friends, not even with Trudy, that had me thinking Gin was in a box with no label. I didn't have one for her, and sometimes that mixed me up. Sometimes, for no reason at all, that made me feel guilty.

Right then, Gin was looking me over like there was something she wanted from me that she'd damn sure never ask for. For the first time since I'd met her, for the smallest second, I wondered what it would be like to push off this stool, take hold of my good friend Gin's face and kiss her like a man kisses a woman who is above labels.

Christ, I bet it'd be sweeter than honey and burn better than the first shot of Jack all the way down.

Just then, the moment ended. Trudy's face—her big blue eyes, her tanned skin, her bleach-blonde hair—came rushing to my mind, and I forgot about what might be and reminded myself of what was.

"There ya go." I pushed the shot back at her. We took it at the same time. I glanced at her, attention on her mouth. The way her throat worked as she swallowed and then I smashed back the Jack, eyes slamming shut.

"Dale, I saw Trudy kissing another man."

The Jack got caught somewhere in the middle of my throat. It stayed there as I lowered the glass, my movements slow and calm. Everything felt foggy, like a fuse had been lit, and I had seconds to move before the bomb ignited.

Gin's eyes were wide as she watched me set the glass on the counter and swallow down the rest of the shot. I hung my arm off the bar as I moved my head just a fraction, looking her over, trying my damnedest to guess if she'd snuck in more Jack than I'd noticed and had gone off the rails.

Keeping my voice as calm as I could muster, I stared right at her, wondering when she'd laugh. Why the hell she'd thought this shit was at all funny. Friend or not, there were just some lines you didn't cross, no matter how funny you think the joke is.

"Gin," I started, my mouth drying up when I caught the way she sat up straight. "That shit ain't funny."

"No," she said.

I'd seen the woman mad before. I'd seen her worried. I'd seen her working through the typical shit that messes with everyone's head at the worst possible moments. But I'd never seen the expression she wore on her face in that instant. It was calm, but concerned, edging on the side of scared. Gin was no coward. Logic told me she wasn't the sort to start shit where there wasn't any. So why the hell would she say something like this about my wife?

"I get that Trudy isn't your favorite person." It wasn't a stretch to say.

Trudy had gotten drunk at the network Christmas party and thought for some fool reason that Kit and Gin were both after me. No matter that Kane and I both promised her there was nothing to whatever bullshit she made up in her head, the woman wouldn't hear it. She cornered both women and made an ass of herself, announcing to the entire crew that I was off-limits to "any bitches with plans on taking" what was hers.

I was still apologizing for that shitshow.

"This has nothing to do with the Christmas party, Dale. I'm not one to hold grudges." I cocked an eyebrow, and she didn't flinch, kept her composure like she dared me to challenge her promise. "Think what you will. You know I'm not that kind of woman. I say what I mean, and I don't make up stories when there aren't any." She emptied what was left of the bottle into our glasses, giving me most of the contents. She pushed my glass toward me as though she thought I'd need it. "Last Tuesday…"

"Tuesday?" My voice went loud, topping above the low steel guitar and Patsy Cline's alto coming from the speakers behind the bar. "You're claiming my wife is stepping out on me, and it takes you a week to fill me in?"

She motioned to the glass, and I took it, ignoring the way she lifted her eyebrows like she wouldn't *finish what she had to say until I was good and buzzed. "Like I was saying, Tuesday, Madison and I were leaving our kickboxing class. We have to use that parking garage on Third."*

I opened my mouth to complain, something I guessed Gin knew I'd do because she held up a finger to silence me. It wouldn't be the first time I'd complained about that parking garage. There'd been four stolen cars and two carjacking attempts in that garage in the past year.

"Like I was saying, you gotta walk a few blocks from the studio to get to the garage." She took her shot, scooting to the edge of her stool. "Gotta pass a few bars. Tuesday is ladies' night at Side Car. There's always a bunch of drunken idiots being obnoxious. Madison likes to make fun of them. I'd just as soon get out of downtown and get myself home."

"You got a point coming anytime soon?"

She was crawling around her story, and the longer she took, the angrier I got. I counted on Gin. I trusted her. Sure, Trudy could be a pain in the ass, but she'd never cheat on me. We'd gone through some rough patches, but she loved me. She'd waited for me on my last deployment. A woman who will wait for you will stay with you.

"Listen to me, Dale," Gin said, her voice getting louder. "I'm not sitting here for my health or to start some sort of drama. You know me better."

"Thought I did."

At that, Gin stood, looking like fire had set between her dark eyes, and the pink splotches on her cheeks that I thought earlier were from her nerves grew darker. A clear sign that her temper was rising. It was a warning I was too stupid to heed.

"You know what? Fine, believe what you want. Think I'm lying? I don't care. But go ask Madison what we saw as we passed that bar, and I swear to you, she'll tell you, just like I am, it was your wife and some suit kissing on her neck, his hands all over her ass as she pulled him against... Well, I'll spare you the details, but it was not just a friendly drink after work." She started to walk away, thought better of it, and turned to face me again. "Strike that. It was the friendliest dang after-work drink I've ever seen in my life. With tongues."

She stood there watching me, her gaze steady, and her mouth in a sharp line. I could only stare back. Out of my control, my jaw clenched, and a thousand different thoughts ran through my head.

Gin was a stand-up woman. She'd never bullshit me. She'd never lied, as far as I could tell, but things had been different since that Christmas party. She'd made it clear she was no fan of Trudy.

Was this her play now?

Making up shit?

Seeing my wife in some woman who might look like her?

Or was I a blind asshole, not seeing the truth right in front of my eyes?

"I don't know where this is coming from," I told her, not sure what to think or how to sort out all the shit clogging up my mind.

"It's the truth, Dale." Gin touched my arm. Her voice was soft and, for a second, I saw what a friend she was to me. "I'm sorry to be the one to tell you, but Trudy is cheating on you."

"You lying bitch!"

Behind Gin, my wife's voice squawked so loudly. She moved so quickly. We both only had warning enough to break apart before Trudy attacked. There were a few seconds of quiet, unbelievable milliseconds of surprise where everything stilled.

Then all hell broke loose.

"You unbelievable cunt! How dare you?" Trudy jumped on Gin like a flea after a fat Yorkie. She pounced, her hands going around Gin's neck before I could stop her.

Gin pivoted back, blocking one of Trudy's hands and those manicured fingernails of hers with her forearms. "Just...having..." Gin panted, pushing Trudy back when she lunged at her again, my wife swinging, moving faster than I could catch her, "my...friend's back!"

"Bitch, please. We both know you just want him on his back!" Trudy screamed, lobbing another swing, which Gin deflected.

I managed to get my arm around my wife's waist, ignoring the scratches she made on my wrist.

"Let me go! I mean it, Dale. Right damn now!"

"Calm the hell down."

"Crazy...bitch," Gin muttered, incensing my wife.

"Shit..." I said, sighing when Trudy stomped on my foot, wiggling away from me, jerking a bony elbow into my gut so sharply that I doubled over. I was only distracted for half a second, but it was half a second long enough for Trudy to lunge again at Gin.

This time, though, the redhead didn't hold back. And when my wife missed, clearly not expecting Gin to do more than weave from the jab, Gin caught Trudy hard right in the jaw, shooting her head back and knocking her off her feet.

Gin stood over my wife as she wailed and screamed on the floor, blood pouring from her mouth. She did a piss-poor job of trying to keep a loosened tooth from falling out of her mouth.

"What the fuck?" I yelled, holding Trudy, torn between trying to calm her and wanting to scream at Gin. I glared up at her, getting more pissed. She didn't look a bit sorry that she'd bloodied up my wife. "What the hell is wrong with you?"

"Me?" Gin asked, widening her eyes. "Are you serious?"

"She's fucking bleeding!"

"She kept swinging at me. What the hell did you expect me to do, stand there and let her throttle me?"

I managed to get Trudy up and off the floor. She held on to me, still carrying on. It was her alone that kept me from screaming at Gin. It was getting my wife cleaned up and looked after that kept me from asking my friend why she'd messed things up between us.

"This is bullshit I never expected from you."

"Yeah." She shook her head like I was the biggest disappointment of her life. "I know the feeling, asshole."

I left the bar with my wife sobbing on my shoulder the entire way to the emergency room.

Two hours later, Trudy lay on the hospital bed, her nose full of gauze and her front tooth missing. I camped out next to her, listening to the rain outside the window drench the city. I'd thought she was asleep. But Trudy was never more motivated than when she was pissed off.

"She wants you, Dale," she'd said, her voice soft, a little defeated.

It tore at my insides to hear my bullheaded wife sound that way.

"You're an idiot if you don't see it." Trudy curled to her side away from me, looking small, her arms shaking.

Couldn't damn well help myself. I went to her, covering her up with a blanket. She grabbed my hand, pulling me onto the bed. I curled around her, still not convinced of anything but how confused I was.

My wife let out a shaky breath and pulled my hand under her chin. "No one goes so far as to lie about their friend's wife cheating if they don't have ulterior motives."

"It ain't like that," I told her, still unable to believe that Gin would stoop to lying. "She's not like that."

"She's a woman, honey. We're all like that."

I should have listened to Trudy then. There was a confession in what she told me that night in the hospital.

But loyalty makes you blind.

Love makes you an idiot.

Truth was, I had no idea about any of it.

The next day, Trudy was released, and I was given an ultimatum: keep away from Gin or lose Trudy.

I was a faithful husband.

I'd been a shitty friend.

Gin didn't speak to me for two weeks after I announced that we couldn't have anything other than job-related discussions.

"Because of your wife?" She narrowed her eyes. I managed a nod, just one, before she shook her head, muttered a low "fucking idiot" under her breath, and knocked my shoulder as she passed me.

Two weeks later, I came home to an empty house and a note Trudy left on the refrigerator.

Dale,
I've outgrown you and am moving on
to better things.
It's over.
That little ginger whore can have you,
Trudy

It rained the night she left. It always rained in the Pacific Northwest, but the rain that night was torrential. The bars had closed, and nothing was open but a 7-Eleven. I spent two hundred dollars on cheap liquor and drove until the white lines on the road became blurry.

I drove until I was sure my truck did most of the navigating on its own.

Until I found myself soaking wet with a bottle of Jim Beam between my knees as I camped out on Gin's front porch.

Thunder cracked against the black sky, and I could see the streets flooding with water. The onslaught flowed into the ditches and storm drains as I leaned against the door, that heavy bottle getting lighter and lighter the longer I sat there.

And just like that, Gin's face hovered in front of me. She didn't smile. She looked, if I were honest, pissed beyond belief. So, I smiled and offered her a swig of my bourbon. The woman shook her head, like I was pathetic and stupid.

She still took a drink.

"You feeling friendless, Hunter?"

"Nah." I grabbed the bottle when she tried to keep it from me. "Feeling cheated on." The bourbon went down smooth but heavy, and I took in a deep breath. "Feeling left by my wife."

The look on her face was one I hated seeing on anyone—pity. I suspected she knew this, likely she saw something of that hatred in my expression. Gin stood, pulling me to my feet, and hustled me inside. She let me lie on her sofa. She even threw a thick quilt over me after she helped me tug off my boots.

Gin didn't even bother trying to take the bottle from me.

"Don't suppose you wanna talk about it," she said, sitting on the floor next to the sofa.

"I do not."

She nodded, fiddling with the tie of her open robe, pretending not to notice me watching her. Her nose was straight, with the smallest bump in the center. For a second, I thought of touching it. I thought of running a finger down the center just to see what it would feel like, but I realized what a dumb thing that was to do.

Hell, I was drunk.

"You were right, and I'm an asshole." I leaned back against the pillow as I handed over the bottle.

She took it, moving it to the coffee table at her side. Then she looked at me, brushing the hair from my face as though it were a favor, not something she did to be sweet. "I didn't want to be."

"No one does when it's bad news." I shut my eyes, kept them closed and grinned, feeling her stare on my face. *"Serves me right."* I hated the whine in my voice, but I was too drunk to care much about it. *"Always figured I'd sinned too much, did too many dirty things to ever be forgiven."*

"Everybody deserves forgiveness, Dale."

"Not everybody." The sofa dipped when she pushed herself up to stand. I caught her hand, bringing it to my mouth as I looked up at her. *"Swear to Christ, I'll never doubt you again."*

"Good," she said, smiling at me. *"I'll hold you to that."*

Back then, all I had left was my honor and the friendship I had with my Gingerbread. Now, I was trying to win both back. She'd been honest. She'd been real with me when I couldn't be real with myself. Right then, as I looked down at her talking to Carelli, as the crew dispersed and the day came to an end, I told myself I'd have to be real with her when I met with her at the diner.

It was the only thing of value I had left.

My cell vibrated again, and I slipped it out of my pocket, irritated when I saw Trudy's text lighting up the screen.

The woman was relentless, I'd give her that. But I didn't have time for her.

I had to think of what I'd say to Gin when I met her. There was a lot to say. I glanced down at the lower roof, phone still in my hand, and caught her watching me. My stomach turned when I spotted the way her gaze shifted from my face to the cell in my hand. When her smile lowered into a frown, I realized it would take more than being real to convince Gin things were different now.

This time, it would take honesty, and I had no intention of waiting to give it to her.

Chapter Ten
Gin

I wasn't looking forward to another greasy meal at Dakota's. It was a nice enough place and I liked Noreen, the older waitress who used milk, not water in the hot chocolate she served me. But meeting Dale, having to sit there and pretend I wasn't seething that he'd shown up uninvited to my set, would be a test of my self-control. And I had very little of that when it came to Dale Hunter.

Inhaling, I checked my appearance one last time in the mirror, fluffing out my hair, then rolling my eyes at myself because I realized I was fluffing my hair and checking my makeup for Dale, whom I was still so pissed at. I hurried to the door, ready to get this little dinner over with. I was a strong woman, I told myself. I could face him and not be weak.

The door was heavy but came open easily when I turned the handle, then my insides liquified. Dale stood on the other side, his arms on the frame, smelling of that delicious rosewood soap he used. He looked like something right out of a *Men's Health* ad in his jeans and snug-fitting Henley.

I am weak, weak, *weak*.

I opened my mouth, but the only sound that left it was a squeak of surprise.

Dale straightened, lifted his hands like he wanted to stop any fussing I'd do before I started. "I'm sorry for showing up like this." I pushed a frown onto my face, though I had to force it there. He shook his head, moving into my room without an invitation. Again, he silenced me, this time by tugging off his jacket like he damn well knew he'd be staying awhile.

Why the hell wasn't I telling him to leave?

"And before you tell me my apologies are no good, or that I'm a piece of shit for going over Carelli's head to get the job, yeah, maybe that's true. But I needed to apologize at the wedding, and the words got all twisted around my tongue, and I couldn't get them out."

"That's no excuse for you to..."

"You were too beautiful."

I stopped speaking, unable to do more than stare at him as he watched me. Dale didn't grin or smirk or make any comment that made me think he was joking. Flattery usually didn't work on me, but Dale never used it. Coming from him, it had me rattled.

He took advantage of my surprise by continuing. "I saw you that first night...looking the way you did, so..." He shook his head, gaze shifting to the window. He rubbed his fingers against his top lip as though he needed a second to decide if what he was saying made sense. Dale's attention was on the activity outside the window—a plane flying far above the cityscape, to the Empire State Building in the distance. But when he spoke, his words were for me alone.

"You were...so... Hell, I'd never seen anyone in my life that beautiful." He watched me, then stepping closer, and I couldn't move. "You made me breathless. Speechless. I didn't know how to react."

I had to force myself to step back. "Well," I finally said when he stood there, staring at me. I had to keep myself busy before I did something epically stupid like lunge at him and devour his mouth. "Well," I repeated, moving to the table next to the window, taking off my own jacket. I needed something to distract myself from his attention, from how closely Dale watched me. I went to the bar, pouring bourbon into a glass, downing a shot before I looked up at him, motioning the bottle at him in silent offer.

"Yeah. Thanks," he said, taking the glass before he followed me to the table and sat.

He took a great gulp of the bourbon and I sipped, too caught up in the way the thick muscles of his neck moved as he drank. His skin was darker than it had been this morning, and the sight of it reminded me he'd manipulated his way onto my set. I'd put him to work doing the job he hated most. That helped to lessen my shock at Dale calling me beautiful. The recall of it made things feel normal again.

"How was the tar work?" I asked, not hiding the humor in my tone.

"Pain in the ass and you know it," he said through a laugh.

I shrugged, hiding my smile behind my glass. "You push, I push back. This is what we do—or what we used to do."

He went quiet. He grabbed the bottle of bourbon from the bar when he'd finished his drink. He nodded, refilling mine before he sat back down. I tried to ignore how good it felt to be here with him. How I liked the familiarity of it. How it felt safe.

Dale cleared his throat, bringing my gaze back up to his face. "The Lake Washington cottage."

"What?"

Dale took slower sips from his drink now, relaxing the more he drank. "You're trying to think of the last time we worked together. It was the cabin in Seattle right after Kit and Kane got together. We were wrapping up that cottage on Lake Washington with the funky pergola by the side porch when Kiel called Kane asking for help with the mafia stalker."

"That's right. We didn't wrap that until you were out of the hospital."

"And you hated me by then."

I looked at Dale, my mouth tight. He had to know why.

Trudy wasn't the only issue. She was a big issue, and he had made it worse with the sweet talk while he was in the hospital. Dale knew why I was still mad at him. I wasn't going to broach the subject.

Besides, he was the one who'd flown all the way from Washington and had a sit-down with a mafia boss to land a spot on my crew. If he wanted to hash out lingering issues, he'd have to bring up why I'd been pissed at him for so long.

"No, I didn't hate you." I wanted him to know the truth. "I was just so...angry."

"And you still are." It wasn't a question.

"Dale."

He set his glass down, moving his elbows to the table. "How long are you gonna punish me for something I had no control over?"

"No con..."

Anger bloomed inside my chest and shot up my neck. If I knew my temper—and I did—I'd bet everything I owned that my face had gone all splotchy and my cheeks were flaming red. I would have taken the opportunity to tell Dale to kiss my ass and fuck off, but at that very moment, the asshole's cell vibrated in his pocket.

He jumped, clearly caught off guard by the interruption. "Sorry," he said, hurrying to silence the call.

I sat back, arms folded as he fumbled with his phone. "This is ridiculous."

Dale jerked his gaze to me, still holding his cell between his fingers.

I leaned forward, palm flat against the table. "What's going on that your attention is so divided? You were like that at the wedding, and today on set, you..."

"Anthony," he said. The name came out in a grunt, as though it took effort for him to admit it.

My temper flared then for a different reason. "You have got to be shitting me."

"I'm not answering the call." Dale slipped his cell back into his pocket, pausing when I glared at him. "What? I'm not lying."

"You want to, though."

He didn't answer.

Something in my chest burned. It prickled and twisted out of some misplaced sense of loyalty for Dale that still lingered inside me. "He's stolen from you. Had you beaten up."

He nodded, fist back against his lips.

There was a line denting the skin between his eyebrows as I spoke, each sentence like an accusation that didn't surprise him. "He is a liar."

Another nod.

"And a cheater."

And another.

Dale had one weakness and only one—his family. His brother and sister were the only two people in the world who made him vulnerable. Jazmine never asked him for anything. She always took care of herself because, as Dale had told me time and again, she was too proud to ask anyone for a thing.

But Anthony was like every other addict I'd ever known. He used people. He took advantage of people. Dale, most of all. And Dale, the strongest, fiercest man I knew, could be toppled by the one syllable from his kid brother he could never refuse—*please.*

"One day, he will ask you for help, and it will get you killed."

Dale closed his eyes, not bothering to look at me. He mumbled under his breath, likely trying to talk himself out of whatever it was he didn't want to say to me.

I picked up my glass but didn't drink. "Addicts are addicts for life."

"I know that." Dale jerked his attention to me. "You think I don't know that?" His voice was loud. The sound echoed like a whip inside the room, making the noise around us pause for a breath. Dale rubbed his face, scratching his nails through his hair before he regrouped. "I know how you feel about them. I know Tony has fucked me over again and again. That's why I haven't taken his call."

"Bottles over babies," I muttered, not meaning to be heard.

Dale made out what I said and reached across the table to grab my hand.

Part of me wanted to jerk away from his touch, dropping my hand into my lap. Another part of me, the part that remembered how good a friend Dale had been, had me pausing.

"Your father didn't deserve you," he said, keeping his voice low. "None of them did."

Billy Sullivan, the man who made me, had left me at a hospital the night of my fifth birthday. He promised the nurse he'd be back to check on me after he had a smoke. Even as a five-year-old, I knew better.

Twelve hours later, I was sent to a foster home, and I stayed in the system until I was eighteen. My father died when I was twenty. I didn't go to his funeral. Never knew who my mother had been. Never had anyone but Ms. Mixen, the last foster mother who took me in at sixteen. She'd been dead by the time I was twenty-four. Killed by a junkie for the thirty-five bucks she had in her wallet one September night in Knoxville.

Addicts, in my experience, wrecked you.

My father had wrecked me.

Anthony would wreck Dale if he let him.

The weight of Dale's hand felt *too* good. I pulled my hand free of his touch, reminding myself of the things he refused to acknowledge.

The most important thing I needed him to remember.

"Well, it's in the past. That man is dead now."

"What I wanted to ask you," he said, his tone different, a smile on his face, "is how far your good grace extends." When I dipped my head, furrowing my eyebrows, Dale elaborated. "You think you'll ever forgive me?"

"Forgive you for what?"

He opened his mouth as though the word skirted the tip of his tongue but got stuck somewhere around the middle. I knew what he'd say before he spoke. He wanted forgiveness for things out of his control. Not for things he seemed so damn adamant not to remember.

Dale inhaled, hesitating before he downed the rest of his glass.

I shook my head. Waved off whatever bullshit excuse he might have surfacing. "Save it."

I left the table, returning the bourbon to the bar. I debated if I should down what remained in the nearly empty bottle or kick Dale out and drown myself in a hot bath.

It seemed, though, that redneck wasn't done with our conversation. I didn't hear him coming up behind me. It wasn't until that rosewood scent hit my sinuses and I felt the heat from his body and spotted his hand resting next to my head on the wall at my side that I realized he stood behind me.

Dale was taller than me by at least four inches. I turned, straightening my shoulders, chin lifted, hoping he caught the *back-off* vibe I pretended I sent out.

"For not telling you what I wanted."

He gave nothing away. No confusion. No real remorse. I hated him, just a little, for the admission. Dale didn't seem sorry at all for never mentioning what happened between us the night of the shooting. "That's...it?"

"That's not enough?"

"No," I said, pushing him back, not wanting him close to me. "No, it's not enough." I turned, hating that there were tears burning my eyes. "You pretend like nothing happened...before."

Dale frowned, his mouth drawing into a firm line that made him look like a confused kid. The expression didn't suit him. "What...do you mean? *Before?*"

"The cabin, Dale. Before Vinnie attacked." When he only stared at me, I stepped back, laughing to myself, but I found nothing funny. "You can't even be bothered to remember what we did..."

"What..." Dale scrubbed his face as though trying to force his head to rewire itself. "There aren't..." He looked up at me, his expression open for the first time I'd ever seen, as though he was truly lost. "I don't have all my memories."

"What are you talking about?" I wiped at my face, irritation burning in my eyes right along with my frustrated tears. "You forgot what you said to Trudy, but everything else..."

"Of course, I forgot what I said to Trudy. You think I went all sweet-mouthed on that crazy woman because I was soft in the head? That medicine messed with me. It fucked me up. But it wasn't just what I said to her. I've got no memory of the attack. I don't remember anything from the time we left set Friday until I woke up in the hospital."

Something deep inside me felt like it uncoiled. Like my insides had just unplugged and all the depleted stores of energy that had barely sustained me the past year slowly began to refuel. I watched him, watched the sincerity and confusion in Dale's expression collide. That sensation redoubled, slowly but surely. It felt like something was stirring; something that felt a lot like cautious hope was coming back to life inside me.

"That's not... Why the hell..."

"You cut me off! Don't you remember? You didn't wanna talk to me. Hell, from what Kane said, you didn't even want to talk *about* me. No one could mention me or tell you what I was up to because you were so..." Tears thickened in my lashes, and Dale moved his gaze, stepping closer, his attention on my face. He grabbed my shoulders, holding me tight. "What happened in that cabin?"

I let a long breath move past my lips. I tried to keep my heart from rattling out of my chest before I spoke. It was too much to wish for, too much to believe that Dale simply didn't know, couldn't remember what had happened between us.

"I..."

He touched my cheek. His thumb stroking along my cheekbone managing to calm me, make me feel safe and sure and settled enough that I was able to speak. "You kissed me."

"That I remember," he said, keeping his focus on my mouth.

"And...kept kissing me." Dale raised one eyebrow, a curious movement that made me think he didn't hate the idea of where my answer was leading. "And, well, that kiss got...um...lower."

Both eyebrows went up then, and Dale's expression relaxed completely.

"How—and I can't fucking believe I have to ask this—but how in God's name does information like this go missing?"

"Completely missing?" I asked, not minding when he moved closer.

He shook his head. The grin he wore transformed, his mouth drawing down until he rested his forehead against mine. "Gingerbread, I can't...I'm so fucking sorry. I'm...I'm sorry." He rubbed the heels of his hands into his eyes and shook his head, like the entire explanation was too impossible, too frustrating to even think about. And then Dale pinched the bridge of his nose before he rested his palm against the wall next to my head. "The first time I kissed you..." he said, his tone going low, the soft cadence in his words reminding me of the growl that had been in his voice that night at the Kaino cabin. "It wasn't...enough."

There wasn't enough space next to this small bar.

He moved closer, and I stopped breathing. "The second time I kissed you...you didn't want it."

Hell. There wasn't enough space on the planet.

Dale took my face in his large hand, moving my chin up. His attention was on my mouth and his thighs were against mine as I gripped his biceps.

"This time, I want it to be more than enough." He leaned down, giving me a small, barely passable kiss. He nibbled on my bottom lip like it was candy. "This time, I want you to want it. I fucking want to remember every damn second."

Dale brushed against me, leaning into me so that I felt the solid angles of his muscular frame. He smelled delicious and felt solid. I couldn't move, couldn't keep anger or recollection of the past in my head, nothing except for this man. The way he smelled, the way he touched me, and how I was desperate for him never to stop doing that very thing.

"Do you want more, Gingerbread?"

"I...why are you...what are you doing to me?"

"Trying to make up for all the times I messed this up." He motioned between us. He lifted his hand to brush back my hair. "Can't say enough how sorry I am for the way I keep doing that." He used those long fingers to cup the side of my face. He leaned down, breath close, heat warming against my lips.

There was a pause, then Dale flicked his gaze to my eyes. One last attempt at a warning I didn't need before he kissed me.

Dale didn't take his time. He didn't savor or tease. His tongue was forceful. His mouth engulfed.

I became a meal that he devoured. My heart pounded and raced so that breathing was something I had to remind myself to do.

He tasted, and I took what he gave. I loved how full he filled my mouth. How he threaded his fingers into my hair and worked his tongue over my lips, controlling, demanding, like he couldn't get enough of the sounds I made or the way I tasted.

"Fuck." He lowered his mouth to my chin, inhaling against my skin. His tongue flirted over my neck as he pulled my shirt away from my shoulder, teeth scraping across my skin. "Want to taste you...*everywhere.*"

I responded to the visual. I was swept up in memory, desire, and the brewing hope that he'd almost been mine for so long. When I curled my fingers in his hair, pulling him closer, Dale's throat vibrated with a deep, moaning growl that made me wet and throbbing and so anxious to feel himself everywhere he wanted to taste me.

He lifted me, reminding me of that night at the cabin. He pulled my legs around his waist as he walked us farther into the room, coming just short of the bed. "You tell me to stop." He held me away from his mouth with his fingers twisted back in my hair. "And I will."

I wished I could read his mind. Understand what the look he gave me meant. It felt a little desperate. It looked a little wild, but I'd spent too many years hoping that what I saw in Dale's face was a truth he'd never admit. He had to come to me. It had to be him directing this.

I'd been his fool one too many times.

I shook my head, not giving him anything. I think he understood I was done with dangling hope. When he kissed my neck, his fingers tugging my shirt farther down my shoulder, I forgot about that hope, foolishness, and the worry over what waited on the other side of this moment.

The only thing on my mind right then was the way he kissed me and how to get him to never stop.

"Lower," I panted, my voice breathy and weak.

It did something to Dale. My words stirred something in him that I'd never seen. The man went after me like he'd been possessed, like my skin was a drug he'd never get enough of.

"Gingerbread," he moaned, licking a path over my shoulder. He pulled my shirt off completely before he tossed it to the floor. "*My* Gingerbread." Gaze on my face, watching, Dale trailed his wet lips across my collarbone. He knelt in front of me, his hands on my back as he glided his mouth over my skin.

My skin ignited at every wet path of fire he stoked in my body with his fingers and tongue. Then he lowered his hands to the small of my back, making me arch up, bringing my breasts forward so that he could tease my cleavage, devour the swells of flesh with his teeth and rough bristles of his beard.

"Dale..." I wheezed, pressing his face deeper, wanting him closer. "More...please...more."

He stopped at my words. Frozen, panting, but didn't take his touch from me. When I worried that he'd changed his mind, Dale inched closer, knowing me well enough to understand disappointment in my features when it appeared.

"I want you, don't think any different." He reached behind me to loosen one of the clasps holding my bra closed with his forefinger and thumb.

"But?" I said, not trusting myself with more than one-syllable words.

Dale licked his lips, gaze running over my face like he wanted to memorize every curve, every dip and bow of my features. "Before...when I didn't have the words..." He swallowed. His expression tightened so that his eyebrows drew together. "Before, I just always figured I wasn't good enough for..." He nodded between us, hand tugging my back to emphasize the closeness between our bodies. "For this, because I was so mixed up."

I watched him. That beautiful, rugged face. The honest expression breaking my heart just a little. My shirt was gone, and only one hook separated my naked breasts from his mouth. We were closer than we'd ever been to changing everything between us.

"And...now?"

"Now..." He moved closer, pulling me closer to the edge of the mattress. "You were gone...this whole time, and now... *Now,* I'm more mixed up without you. This time, baby, it will be different. We'll be different." Dale didn't move. He seemed to wait for me like he wanted permission to push us both over the cliff.

I jumped first.

His wide arms were wrapped around me, not moving.

I nodded, reaching behind my back to unfasten the last clasp.

Dale had the perfect poker face, stoic and straight. He used it then, making it impossible for me to read what he thought.

I reached up to lower the lace fabric from my breasts and took off my bra.

His attention flicked to the round swells of my breasts before he held them. He pulled one nipple into his mouth, then between his teeth, tongue teasing, working it to a peak that had me wet and curling around him, locking my ankles around his waist.

"Dale...shit...oh God..."

"You...want more?" he asked, voice a low, gravelly tone.

The vibration was a sweet tease against my skin.

I pulled up his face. Done with everything but taking what I wanted. Done with wanting and having nothing. Done with aching and never being full. Dale watched me. That gruff, trained composure only fracturing when my breathy words came out on one exhale. "I want all of you."

Those full, wet lips opened a fraction as his eyes went hard, lighting with something that reminded me of a thunderstorm.

He looked hungry and ready to devour me whole.

"Good." He lifted to kiss me like my lips were oxygen and the last breath was leaving his lungs. "Because I'm going to take everything you've got."

Dale pushed me back, standing with one foot on the floor and a knee on the mattress. He took my ankle, slipping off my skirt and panties. The whole while keeping his gaze on my face and his grip tight on my body. He was calculating, showing me with every graze of his lips against my ankle, my calf, the inside of my thigh, how calm he could be.

When he slipped closer, leaning over me, resting on his elbow, I followed his lead. I returned the stare he gave me as he directed my leg over his shoulder, spreading wide for him when he pushed my knees apart.

"Ginger everywhere," he mumbled against my pink skin, licking the length of my pussy. He held me steady, tongue wet and strong as I arched into his mouth. He worked me over, up, the frenzy overwhelming. The air around us thickened with my moans, my growling pleasure.

"Like that...*yes*..." I tugged on his hair, fingers twirling his long waves. He read my body, stroked deeper, longer, slipped two fingers inside me the louder my moans became, the shallower my pants grew. And then I soared and crested, coming hard. My hips lifted as Dale finger-fucked me, held on tight, pulling his mouth away. I blinked to find his sharp gaze on me and an easy, satisfied grin softening those sweet, rough features.

"My Gingerbread." He sounded awed as his hand slipped up my thigh. "So beautiful."

I couldn't wait. I didn't want the moment to pass me by. I went after Dale, surprising him by sitting up, tugging him close to take his mouth. With his collar between my fingers, breath fanning out against his face, I claimed his mouth as badly as I wanted to claim his body.

"Gin..." he tried, but I couldn't take the chance that he would try to stop me.

There had been too many close calls.

Too many distractions.

"I want to see you." I silenced the unflappable SEAL with five small words.

Dale nodded once, letting me strip him. He offered no resistance when I tugged off his long pullover, kissing every inch of perfectly taut muscle I saw. He leaned back, hands on the back of my head when I loosened his belt and went for his zipper, dragging down his jeans.

I'd never seen him so still. He'd never been this quiet. The way he watched me, how curious and observant he was, reminded me of a negotiator trying to talk a man off the ledge of a forty-story building.

But the only jumping I'd do, Dale would follow.

The mattress dipped when I left the bed to rid him of his boots. Still, Dale didn't move. He was hard. Ready for me. That mammoth bulge tenting the black shorts he wore as I crawled across the bed, kissing his stomach.

"Gin...I don't expect you to..."

"I told you." He held his breath when I licked just above his waistband. "Tonight, I want all of you."

Dale's throat bobbed, and he dropped his head back when I pulled him out, marveling at the length and size of him. He was wide, thick, and pulsing in my hand. I took him whole, licking the tip, wanting to relish all he had, but I was only able to manage to go slow.

"Christ." He gripped the duvet in each hand as I sucked him. His chest worked double time the more I swallowed around him. When I cupped him, using one hand to stroke him as I sucked, Dale released the duvet to clutch the back of my head, breath coming faster and faster.

He filled me up. Just this. Dale in my mouth. His smell all around me. His heat on my skin and the memory of his tongue and fingers and the strong, wild orgasm he gave me still humming between my legs.

I could leave right now and be happy.

Not satisfied completely, but happy.

I wanted it all.

When I looked at him, licked around the tip, rubbing it against my bottom lip, Dale shook his head, looking torn between being turned on and half crazed by what I did to him. "Devil woman."

"Guilty." I flicked my tongue over the tip before I sucked him all the way into my mouth again.

"Come here, Gingerbread." The look he gave me told me well enough that he'd fallen over to half crazed. "Now, baby."

I leaned up, slipping over his thighs, sweeping my nails over his beautiful chest, down his stomach, thinking he'd let me play.

But Dale didn't seem to be in the playing mood.

The games, it appeared, were over.

He reached for me, hand on my hip as he took my wrist, guiding my hand to his cock. "Take me. Slip me inside you," he said, voice even, control level. Dale was beautiful in that moment. He stared up at me as if he knew all he had, I'd take. As if he'd give me anything I wanted and would always have more for me.

My movements were slow, precise, and we worked together—him releasing my hand when I stroked him. Me sliding up the mattress to position myself over him. Him lifting his legs to steady me as I rose up and sank back down, taking him inch by inch.

"Baby...holy hell, you fit me..." He held my hips, directing me, guiding my movements.

"Perfect," I whispered, understanding what he meant.

I did fit him.

We moved together like we always had, like a dance. Shadow and light, working in time with each other because that's how we'd always existed together.

"So damn perfect."

And it was. It always would be. I had never doubted how Dale would love me or how I'd love him.

We just...worked.

This would work.

I knew it in my bones.

"Harder, Gin. I need you..." He went silent, his grip on my hips tightening when I increased my pace, my pussy getting wetter. Dale let out a low, gravelly groan. "Too much."

"Shit!" I yelped when he grabbed me around the waist and flipped our positions, settling me on my back.

"Hell." His eyes tightened and he leaned back, coming to his palms over me before he dove at my mouth, taking it, kissing me hard. Tongue and lips working together to attack and turn on and overtake.

I let him, meeting him with my hips and my mouth, opening my knees wider and wider just to feel Dale as deep as he could be inside me.

"Christ, baby..." He stretched up, arms shaking but steady. Dale gripped my leg, holding my knee as he pumped into me. He watched my face, his hand against my cheek, his thumb along my bottom lip. "Tighten, baby. Squeeze me." And when I complied, Dale's eyes drifted up, the straight shot of pleasure crossing his features.

I was overcome. So lost in the feel of him that I squeezed tighter and touched myself. My eyes slammed shut as I circled my clit, then shot open when Dale brushed my hand away.

"That's my job." He kissed me, sucking on my bottom lip. "Mine." And when he focused, thumb working, cock throbbing as he moved his hips, my pussy clenched. A rush barreled through my body until I came, squeezing even tighter.

"God..." I breathed, body languid, exhausted, then electrified as Dale moved faster. I held him close, taking his broken breaths, his strangled pants as he spilled himself over and over inside me.

We lay there, Dale still inside me, our bodies sticky, our heartbeats slowing, and I couldn't feel anything but my thumping pulse and the tickle of my hair as he breathed against my neck.

I thought he had fallen asleep, it had been so long. He was still hard, still draped across me. I was too sated, too mesmerized to move. If I did, I was scared the entire night would have been a dream.

Dale lifted up, coming to his elbows to look down at me. His fingers brushed against my face. I wanted to ask what he thought when he looked at me that way.

Seemed to me, since the night of the party, he'd been looking at me that way a lot, but I still didn't have the courage to ask him. Naked with him inside me and I still didn't ask why he looked at me the way he was right then.

"What?" I managed when he grinned at me.

Dale kissed me, slow and perfect before he spoke, hand sliding down my body. "I could *live* inside you. Always."

I wished he would.
God, how I wished he would.

Chapter Eleven
Gin

Dale sang in the shower. The steam billowed from the half-closed bathroom door as I grinned like an idiot, listening to the worst out-of-tune rendition of Aretha Franklin's "Chain of Fools" I'd ever heard. He was in a good mood and taking longer than normal to clean up after the long night we'd had.

"Roll over," he'd told me not two hours ago when my alarm sounded and I was about to leave the bed. The new work schedule I'd assigned myself was unpredictable, likely overkill since we only had ourselves to answer to, but I didn't like keeping things inconsistent. Six a.m. would always be my wake-up call.

"Why?" My limbs still ached from how pleasantly used my body felt.

"*This* is why." Then Dale moved his hips, grinding his hard dick against my ass, before showing me how he'd use me again and again whenever he woke, whenever he thought about it, whenever I did.

The bottom would fall out. I knew that. It always did. But right in that moment, I listened to Dale's horrible singing voice and enjoyed how my body still hummed. How I'd managed to push back all the things he hadn't mentioned. What he'd said to me. What it meant. Him not remembering was one thing. Him telling me what he felt now was something else. I needed the words. But at least things were starting, and I'd take that even if it was all I could get.

My mouth ached from the stupid smile pulling my lips. It only dimmed when my cell rang, the ringtone set to *The Godfather* theme. It was common, stupid, done only to annoy Johnny, but I was glad I'd made it specific to his number.

"Hey," I answered, leaning my head toward the half-opened bathroom door. I got up, hoping Dale didn't hear the small click it made when I closed it.

"What was that racket?"

"Um, one of the maids thinks she's Aretha."

"Well, she sucks. Ah...hold on, *bella*." There was a noise on the other end and then a scratching sound, as though Johnny had covered the receiver. "Listen, we're going to change the schedule today. You up for a farmers market? David has an idea for a remote shoot and wants you to check out one of the vendors this morning."

From the bathroom, Dale hit a high note. I moved to the other side of the room, stepping out onto the balcony. "Yeah," I answered, glancing at my watch. "When do you need me?"

"In a couple hours? It's just a meeting, then we'll do an afternoon shoot at two. I'll get Angelo to tell the crew. You're good with that, *si?*"

"Yeah, of course. No problem."

"Good. I'll pick you up at ten, then."

"No," I hurried to say, though I didn't know why. Johnny was my boss, not my lover. I owed him nothing but my gratitude and a hard day's work. "I...ah, have an errand to run on that side of the city. I'll meet you at the set office. We can leave from there."

"Whatever you want, *tesoro.* See you then."

When I returned inside, Dale was still performing, but he'd moved on to Chris Stapleton, tackling "Tennessee Whiskey" with such abandon, I wished I had a bottle to block out the noise.

The small internal joke didn't amuse me for long. I'd lied to Johnny for no real reason. There was no errand. No explanation for me not telling him who I was with and why I didn't want him to pick me up. He clearly didn't like Dale. God knew, Dale didn't like him. Maybe it was some sort of alpha male territorial bullshit thing between them that caused this mutual hate. Maybe it was because they both claimed to want me. Though, Dale certainly had proven he did over and over again last night.

Still, something niggled in my head, had me asking myself why I'd kept what happened to myself. I didn't feel guilty about being with Dale. I didn't think Johnny would be seriously disappointed.

So why did I lie about it?

That question absorbed my attention as I walked away from the balcony, kept it as I went to the closet trying to decide what I should wear that day. So when Dale's cell vibrated, it took several minutes for me to hear it.

I should have ignored it, like he did. It wasn't my business how often his kid brother texted him. It didn't matter what the guy said or how many times he asked Dale for a rescue. He'd promised he wasn't going to buy the shit his brother was throwing at him.

But that same niggling voice that had me asking myself why I'd lied to Johnny told me there was something different about the flow of messages that landed on Dale's phone. One after another, then another as Dale continued his shower. They came in rapid succession, and I told myself it was that flurry and what might be behind it that made me look.

It was the second lie I'd told myself in under five minutes.

He hadn't changed his phone's passcode in the time I'd known him. Likely, he'd not changed it since he was active in the SEALs. His stepmom's birthday: 060562.

I tried it.

The phone unlocked immediately, and when the screen opened and I swiped my thumb across it, nine messages accompanied the five letters I hated most in the world.

Trudy.

Please answer me, Dale.

You can't ignore me forever.

Sometimes, things aren't about you, and you know it.

Come on, this is serious! Life and death serious!

This time, things are bad. Worse than they've ever been.

I'm trying to help.

Where are you???

You can't say you love someone and pretend they mean nothing. Love doesn't work that way, honey.

And then the last message, the one that made my stomach drop. The one that told me what a mistake it had been to believe that someone like Trudy would ever disappear completely.

I threw the phone down when I read the very last of Trudy's messages. I was convinced she had not let go of Dale. Knowing who he was and how important it was for him to do the honorable thing, he probably wouldn't let go of her either.

"I'd do anything for you," he'd told me when he'd thought I wasn't listening. Then, "You gotta know... you're the only one who matters to me" when he knew I was.

I heard that so clearly in my mind and every utterance of those words ripped through my heart. Now, I knew. He'd said it to me so many times before, and I'd stupidly forgotten how much he meant it and how true it was.

Words really were just words.

They meant nothing.

Before I could convince myself that any excuse he gave me would explain away why he was still in contact with her, I hurried to the closet, throwing on a pair of jeans, my leather boots, and a thick wool sweater and scarf before I tore out of the room, leaving Dale in that bathroom, alone in my hotel room.

I wouldn't film today. I'd tell Johnny we'd start over tomorrow.

Today would be a time for distance.

Distance from Dale and the words his wife had used to convince him how much they still needed each other.

Try to push aside your anger and think about the baby. This isn't her fault.

"That fucker has a vicious right hook." Johnny winced when Angelo reached for his face, aiming to examine the already purple bruise forming along his jaw.

Chapter Twelve
Gin

"Did I apologize?" I lowered my head, covering my face.

Angelo cursed for what must have been the fifth time as he stared at his boss's injury. "Really," I continued, glancing between the two men, "I *am* sorry. I had no idea he'd be so..."

"Possessive?" Johnny asked.

The word was accurate. I pushed down the swell of heat that bubbled in my stomach at the scene that had played out on set this morning—Johnny and Dale fighting. Actually fighting in front of our crew, on our set, because I'd gone AWOL. Because Dale couldn't handle me giving him the silent treatment.

Because he clearly had a child he neglected to tell me about.

And Johnny Carelli got sucker-punched because Dale wouldn't listen when security tried to make him leave the set.

Shit, I felt like a drama magnet.

"I wouldn't say *possessive*, really." The joke was lame, and I couldn't make myself look at Angelo when he sent me a glare.

Johnny caught the look, clicking his tongue before he muttered something low and admonishing to his guard in Italian, sending the man out of the room. "Forgive him." Johnny poured me another glass of wine. "Angelo is protective." He toasted me when I picked up my glass.

Johnny's housekeeper, a thicker woman with graying hair sporting a uniform and a beautiful smile, replaced the wine in the decanter and set two plates in front of us.

"*Grazie,* Mina," Johnny told the woman, grinning when she patted his shoulder.

She walked out of Johnny's sun-room and into his luxury apartment, leaving us alone to eat the impromptu meal she'd made.

"She dotes on you, doesn't she?" I asked, anxious for a subject that would relieve me of some of my guilt, if only momentarily.

The woman had ushered me into Johnny's home when we arrived. She'd asked four times if I was hungry, told me I was too skinny, and then insisted on feeding both of us.

"She does, I'll admit." He watched her disappear into the living room then out of sight before he looked back at me. "She's the niece of the woman who helped raise Cara and me. God rest. My father has a staff who are loyal. Sending her to me, I suspect my father thought, would keep me from eating all my meals at Demonte's."

I grinned, remembering the little dive bar Johnny had brought me to my first night in New York. There were too many men trying to flirt with me, most of them over sixty, but they made up a big group of roughnecks who were union that Johnny had hired for the crew. He'd seemed at home there, and it showed.

"Anyway, all my father's staff think I need a wife." He took a sip, motioning to my plate as he started in on his. "I'm not in the market..." Johnny took a bite of his chicken Marsala, releasing a moan. "But, *merda,* if she cooks like this, I might make an exception."

I hurried to swallow more wine, smelling the delicious garlic wafting in the sauce, and the plump mushrooms and tender chicken of my own dish. "I'll have to find a kickboxing class here in the city." I took a bite and closed my eyes when all those delicious flavors hit my mouth. "And do three extra classes."

"That sounds like you're staying." Johnny stared at me, abandoning his meal.

I copied him, not sure what to make of his expression.

I'd never thought about my plans beyond this shoot and packaging several episodes to present to the studios we planned to pitch the show to. A month, maybe two, was all I'd planned on. I hadn't even thought about finding a place to rent, but things were going well. I liked New York. I liked the crew. I liked almost everything about being here and doing this job.

Except who wouldn't be here if I stayed.

"I don't... God, I wish I knew. Everything is so..." I glanced at Johnny, my attention shooting straight to his purple jaw again. Guilt returned in a flood inside my chest. "I did apologize, right?"

"Bella," he said through a sigh. "I have to say, I'm not surprised. Hunter is a bastard with a wicked right hook, but he isn't stupid, and if I found myself in his shoes..." Johnny stopped there, narrowing his eyes as he shrugged. "Not for nothing, Italian leather, designer shoes, but his shoes nonetheless, then *si*, maybe I would have clocked some *chooch* I thought was trying to lay claim to the woman I thought was mine."

"This is a mess," I whispered, hoping the rim of my wineglass covered the groan in my words.

And it was a mess, an unmitigated disaster of my own creation.

I'd left Dale alone in my hotel room after reading Trudy's messages. He'd have known I'd read them. They'd been new. He would have seen his phone on the bed where I left it. He would have seen the messaging app open the second he unlocked his phone. Seen the messages he hadn't read had been read by someone.

Since I was the only person in the room, the resulting conclusion was obvious.

I hadn't returned, despite how many times he called me. Despite the endless messages. Despite how my body ached from the memory of him over me, in me. I'd left and stayed gone. Didn't bother returning to the set. I'd ignored him completely, and by two o'clock, I turned off my phone and spent the night at Cara's empty apartment, telling Johnny I wanted to take advantage of the spa in the building.

So when we returned to the set this morning and Dale showed up a half an hour later, Johnny was completely unaware that anything had happened between us. All he knew was that Dale was mad. That he looked a little unhinged, and that he directed all his tired energy at me the second he spotted me.

"There a reason he thought that?" Johnny asked, leaning back in his chair.

"Thought what?" I asked, watching him, distracted as the image of Dale's wide, intense eyes came back to me.

I'd never seen him that angry or that desperate to be heard.

"Hunter. Why did he act like I was trying to steal his woman?"

You have to listen to me, Dale had started, *ignoring Johnny at my side and David as he and his producer stared at Dale and how quickly he cornered me. There had been bags under his eyes and red* streaks lining the whites and around the iris. *"I spent all day and night looking for you."*

"This isn't the time or place," I'd said, dismissing him.

"Gin, you got it wrong..."

"Yeah." I didn't look at him, finally realizing that the gleam of hope our night together had given me was a flicker, not a flame. *"I got a lot of things wrong."* Even that small spark was ash now.

"*Bella*?" Johnny leaned against the table as I stared at nothing.

My eyes burned as I remembered the twitch that took over Dale's cheek when Johnny had grabbed his arm as Dale reached for me.

"Hmm?"

"You and Hunter?"

"Oh," I said, finishing off the wine, my voice flat. "Because, Johnny..." I looked at him across the table, drying my face when the tears spilled. *Johnny pushed Dale first. You don't do that to a SEAL. It could be deadly. Dale reacted.* "I slept with him."

I don't know what I expected. Johnny Carelli was a dangerous man. He could be scary, given the right circumstances. I'm sure if there was a woman he wanted to claim, he could be jealous and controlling.

But Cara had shared that her brother and his friends had no interest in keeping company with the same woman for more than a night. In fact, they tended to spread the wealth when it came to beautiful women.

That wasn't my style.

But even if I wasn't Johnny's woman and he didn't have any interest in changing that, he still seemed irritated by my admission. I spotted the tight line that stretched across his mouth as he watched me, absorbing my confession like a sour olive.

"You're disappointed," I said, surprised.

He didn't deny it. He kept his focus on my face, finally relaxing his features so that his mouth eased into a smile. "I think your standards are too low." When I lifted my eyebrows, Johnny shrugged, moving closer to the table, the flame from the candles in the centerpiece throwing soft light around his beautiful face. "You deserve someone who will spoil you, *bella*. Someone who will give you the world."

"I'm fine with acquiring that on my own, Mr. Carelli."

His grin widened, and Johnny waved his hand. A surrender to my will that I was sure by now he would have gotten used to. "Fair enough, but I think you underestimate my intentions."

"Are you talking about your angle?"

"I have angles?"

"Forgotten already?"

He poured another round between us. "You'll have to forgive me. I was injured today by some asshole."

"I seem to recall you explaining all men have angles."

He filled my glass, motioning for me to drink, and I accepted.

"All men, according to you, are plotting things. Typically, nefarious, filthy things, I'm guessing."

Johnny considered my words as he sipped his wine. I didn't know what to make of the wolfish smile he tried to hide behind his glass. "Well." He licked his lips. The motion distracted me enough that, for a second, my bad mood lifted, and I forgot about Dale punching Johnny and Johnny kicking him off the crew. "I'll admit my angles can be filthy, but you, *tesoro*, I make exceptions for."

"And why is that?" I sat back, relaxing even more when Johnny came to my side of the table, kneeling next to me.

He took my hand, bringing it to his mouth. "You are special, Ms. Sullivan, truly rare. And I only love the rarest of treasures."

My mind told me to leave this place. There was nothing here for me.

Johnny Carelli wasn't someone to play with. He couldn't be trusted. He was plotting things I didn't want to be part of. He wasn't what I needed.

So why couldn't I make myself stand up? Why was I becoming so fascinated by the smooth arch of his thick eyebrows and the wide bridge of his nose? Why did the small, dark freckle underneath his left eye grab my attention? Why did the sudden image of Johnny out of that designer suit, a thin smattering of black hair over his chest, and the carefully arranged dark waves of his hair tousled against his pillow hold such fascination for me?

"I'm not...that's not..." I swallowed, my throat going dry. I nodded a dismissive thanks at Johnny when he handed me my glass.

He was affecting me, and he knew it. He likely enjoyed the effect his presence, his handsome face, and expensive cologne were having on me. The bastard was good. Too damn good.

"We...could be good together, my little spitfire."

"Johnny," I warned when he leaned close.

"You and me, *bella,* the things we could do..." He touched my face, the flat of his thumb sliding across my cheekbone. "I could make you forget everyone else." He moved in, making me hold my breath.

I curled my fingers around the arm of my chair as he pressed his thick, warm lips to my forehead.

"Tomorrow night, I will take you to dinner. It will be our first date." When I didn't respond, still hadn't unwrapped my fingers from the chair, Johnny grinned, laughing under his breath. "You think on it, spitfire, and let me know."

Then Johnny stood, taking my hand to lead me out of his apartment and down to the parking garage. He walked me all the way to the waiting limo and once again kissed my forehead as he told me goodnight. It wasn't until we'd cleared the garage and were halfway to my hotel that I realized I was heading right into the lion's den.

Chapter Thirteen

Dale

She never worked this late back in Seattle. Neither did Kit.

Not once. Six o'clock rolled around, and things shut down. That was a rule the network put into place because they were family-oriented. Whatever Carelli was trying to do wasn't, because it was a mafia-funded gig.

There was a family involved, but not a good one.

The elevator chimed, and for the fifth time in more than two hours. I jerked my attention down the hall, irritated when the guys I'd seen leave earlier returned with white bags that smelled like Greek food tucked under their arms. They nodded at me, and I didn't bother to give them one back. Didn't much care if they'd planned on hauling security up here to get me to leave. Turns out when you wear a Navy T-shirt that's probably a size too small, and you tear off your jacket when you're pissed off and sweating because of it, and everyone around you gets a good look at you... well, hell. Suppose it's good enough to look *don't-fuck-with-me* sometimes. Especially when you aren't in the mood to be fucked with.

At least, that was the running theory.

Carelli had a steel jaw. I told myself that asshole hadn't hurt me when I'd clocked him, and he didn't. Much. But what tore me up more than anything was the look on Gin's face when I tried to explain the shit she'd thought she read from Trudy's message.

Think about the baby.

Fucking hell. That little face flashed into my head, and guilt crowded me, crushing my insides like they'd been struck by an anvil. She was too young. Too beautiful and if I had to choose between her and Gin... damn. I knew the choice I had to make.

Hand in my hair, elbows on my knees, I didn't bother looking up when the elevator bell signaled, sure that it wouldn't be her. I'd spent two hours in this hallway. All kinds of scenarios of where Gin had been and with whom swirling in my head. They ran the gamut. They were stupid and horrible, vomit-inducing and disturbing. None gave me comfort. None did one damn bit of good when all I needed was a five-minute conversation to explain what had been going on over the past year with my ex-wife.

"Why are you here?"

I jerked my head up, climbing to my feet to stand in front of her. Christ, she was beautiful and so fucking pissed off at me. One glance at her red-blotched face told me that.

"You need to leave."

"That ain't happening," I said, trying not to grin like a fool when I spotted the way she kept slipping her attention to my arms, then back over my chest. She might be mad, but I knew damn well Gin was thinking about us together in the room right behind this door.

"I don't have anything to say to you," she started, moving the keycard into the lock.

"Good," I tried, holding my hand against the door when she opened it. "Because I want you to listen to me."

"No."

But she walked past the threshold, and I followed, closing the door with my foot, coming behind her as she moved inside.

The room had been cleaned, but from where she'd kept her bags and the planner left open to the same page it had been when I'd left the morning she disappeared on me, I could tell she hadn't been back here.

I closed my eyes, telling myself I wouldn't ask the question.

Telling myself I had no right to know.

Telling myself it would do no good to know the answer.

Hell. I couldn't help it.

"You fuck Carelli?" I turned to face her.

She was in the middle of taking off her necklace but stopped, holding her hands behind her neck to jerk a glare at me. "Excuse me?"

The question was already out there. No sense in taking it back.

I'd had Gin in this room two days ago. She gave me everything she had. She'd taken everything from me. What she did to me, what she let me do to her, that didn't come easy. That wasn't simple. That shit was real and raw and couldn't be forced. It wasn't pretend. No way she didn't feel what I did.

I had to know the truth.

Two steps had me in front of her as she dropped her hands. I ignored the fire blazing bright in her eyes as that glare turned into venom. I'd be a dead asshole if that look were lethal.

"You and Carelli, last night. You let him fuck you?"

Gin opened her mouth, rage cresting and full as she watched me. I knew this woman. She'd been my best friend for years. Her warnings were easy to make out. Right then, she jumped over annoyed, maybe even pissed, and landed right on "You are dead to me." But she'd have to get over it.

I wanted the truth.

"That isn't your business."

"Like hell."

"It. Ain't," she said, that East Tennessee showing up as she curled her top lip and pushed me aside to get into her closet. She didn't care that I watched as she shimmied out of her skirt and shirt like she forgot that undressing in front of me wasn't something we always did. "Last time I checked," she said, standing in front of a mess of clothes she didn't seem to see at all as she flipped through the hangers in nothing but her bra and panties, "I wasn't anyone's wife, didn't belong to a blessed soul. You and I, Mr. Dale *Damn* Hunter, at one time, *were* just friends."

"Were?" I came up behind her.

Gin turned, brushing past me as she abandoned her search for something to wear. "I didn't stutter. *Were*. As in, once was. As in, we ain't now. As in, go home and stop asking me questions that aren't your damn business. We aren't friends. We aren't...any damn thing anymore."

The words registered. I heard them well enough.

Maybe even comprehension was a thing that clicked and fired in my brain. That didn't mean it made much sense to me. That damn well didn't mean I liked it one bit.

Gin's eyes burned bright and glistened as I came at her. Then widened when I grabbed her, tugging her against me. My arm around her waist and my fingers stretched over her ass as I held her off the floor. "That is where you're fucking wrong."

She tried to argue. She at least released a loud sound of protest, but it got stifled by my tongue invading her mouth and the high shrieks of her moans as I pushed my hand between us, carrying her to the bed with my hand on her pussy, teasing, finding her already soaked and getting wetter.

Gin shuddered against my hand. I pushed her to the mattress, moving my hand away long enough to slide it into her panties, slipping two fingers inside her, groaning when she tightened around me. I hovered over her, wanting to taste her everywhere, but so hungry to be inside her, to remind her what was hers, what I had taken from her, what she'd always have of me.

"This," I said, taking my hand away from her, bringing it to my mouth, "doesn't feel like we aren't any damn thing, Gingerbread." Her breathing quickened when I sucked the two fingers, still warm from her pussy, into my mouth.

"Dale..." she breathed, pulling me close like she'd forgotten her anger. Forgotten everything but what her body told her she needed.

"You want me, baby?"

Her nod was hesitant, like she damn well didn't want to admit she wanted anything from me at all. But she kept at my neck, pulling me closer.

I held her wrist to stop her. "I want you. I want all of you too." I took her mouth because it belonged to me and gave her my tongue. Her taste and mine mingling until she moved against me, until she threaded the fingers on both of our hands together and directed them to her clit. I could smell her everywhere. Felt the heat from her body, from her sweet, soft pussy against my leg. Felt the breaking sob of the passionate cries she made and could not take another second of not being inside her.

"Please," she said, sounding ready to burst. "Please, baby…"

Gin kicked off her panties when I got them to her ankles and helped me tug down my jeans and shorts. We tangled together, hands and fingers and needy touches that felt greedy and desperate until I found her. My cock sank into that wet, tight heat, and we both breathed loud gasps of relief when I was inside her.

"You tell me I'm not nothing," I demanded, holding her open with my hand on the back of her knee. Gin arched up, coming up on her elbows as I moved deeper, gripping the pillow over her head, pushing myself deeper inside her. "Tell me. I need you to say it."

"Please…" She stretched, neck twisting to the side when I sucked her nipple into my mouth, wetting the fabric of her bra because I was desperate. I needed to hear her claim me.

"Tell me…"

"You're…oh God…" I redoubled, using both hands now to stretch my Gingerbread farther apart. A whip of pleasure and my own orgasm shot through me when she came, wetness covering both of us. "Oh, baby, you're everything...*fucking* everything."

Later, Gin curled against me, her back pressed to my chest, her hair tangled between my fingers as we listened to the noise of the city through the open balcony door. The darkness and gust of cold air reminded me of something I couldn't place. That same nagging glitch of unconfirmed memory that would unwind from my head over the past year. Something about the night I was shot uncurling in my mind but never letting me get a good look at it.

Right then, I didn't much care what it was. Right then, I was as happy as I could be. As happy as I could get without explaining anything to Gin. I didn't want to ruin the moment. I didn't want to disturb anything. She was pressed against me, and we were good.

Of course, it wouldn't last.

The ring came in three quick successions. I reached across to the foot of the mattress, ready to grab my cell out of my jeans pocket and power it off. It had caused too much shit already, and I didn't want the small peace we had to end.

Gin was faster. Moved before I could.

She answered.

"What do you want?"

The expression on her face told me all I needed to know about who was on the other end. It was enough. It was everything. Trudy had done a lot of damage, but

I'd done more. I kept doing damage to this woman at every turn.

"Is that right?" Gin said, her back to me, the sheets around her body as she faced the window.

She was beautiful with the sunlight coming across her pale skin. Beautiful. Radiant and I wanted her. But I learned a long time ago that when your sins were as plentiful as mine, you didn't always get what you wanted. You usually got what you deserved. I didn't deserve her.

"I'll tell him," she said, ending the call. She held my phone in her hand but didn't turn, kept her attention on the skyline outside that window, her features blank as though there wasn't much more that could shake her. Everything had.

"Gin..." I tried, but I went quiet when glanced over her shoulder, looking my way, but not seeing me.

"Do you love me?"

I closed my eyes, needing a half a second. I inhaled to keep the smell of her in my senses. It would have to keep me. Might never smell it again.

"Gingerbread..."

I knew the second she gave up on me. The tightness in her body relaxed, and everything she held—her breath, probably her hope—it all got lost in whatever thoughts screwed her up and made her think it wasn't in me to want forever with her.

I might not be able to get the words out because of what Trudy had laid on me. I might be holding myself back because of the choices I had to make, but something big still burned bright inside me for this woman.

I'd done so many things I wouldn't ever be forgiven for. There were some sins too dark to ever see the light of forgiveness. For years, Gin had been the only bright spot in my life. I'd just been so damn petrified of dimming that light. Loving me would cost her because I couldn't be what she wanted, especially now. Especially since there wasn't just me to consider.

"I'm tired, Dale. I'm tired of waiting on a man who can't love me back." She moved away from the window, slowly dressing, like there wasn't a rush to get where she was going.

I knew my best friend. She wasn't waiting on anyone, least of all me. She was done. Checked out. It was time I let her go. It was the last thing in the world I wanted and the only thing fair enough for her.

When she was dressed, Gin sat on the mattress and held my face between her fingers. "Whatever happens to you, I hope you get a happy ending." I wanted to tell her the only way that would happen for me was with her. I wanted to stop her, make her stay. I wanted it to be me and Gin and no one else. But that wouldn't be fair. It wouldn't be right. She started to pull away from me, and I gripped the back of her neck, pouring everything I felt, everything I had in me for her into the kiss I gave her. It rattled me, made the ending of that kiss feel like a small death. Gin blinked, her lips swollen and damp before she looked over my face. "Trudy's waiting for you downstairs," she said before she left the bed and me alone in that room.

Chapter Fourteen
Gin

Almost, maybes, and impossible hopes.

That was all I had left.

The almost moments of being with Dale, of loving him with everything I was, anything I would be, was exhausting. Especially when that almost led to never. Maybes were a tease not fit for anyone. Maybes were just no's disguised in glitter that pretended to be gold.

Impossible hopes? That was my bread and butter, and I'd had enough for one lifetime.

How could he touch me, take me the way he had, be that open, that raw with me, show me everything he was, and still keep so much from me? A better question would be, why the hell was I continuing to expect him not to?

It didn't matter, none of it. Trudy's call this morning had been the nail in the coffin. She'd never change, and she'd never be out of his life. I could handle Dale having a child. Just not Dale having a child with that woman.

"If you're done fucking my husband, tell him I'm here to see him."

"Is that right?" I asked, my body still aching from where Dale had been just hours before. When he couldn't tell me he loved me back—the only thing I needed to hear, the only thing that would make dealing with Trudy worth the trouble, that was when I'd had my fill.

I wasn't filming today. The crew worked hard, getting the renovation underway so that Ethan, the lead carpenter/pretty-boy secondary host, could film some how-to segments on project construction. I was supposed to be in a design meeting with Jess, but I skipped it, figuring she could handle the small team better than I could. I'd never done it before because it wasn't in my wheelhouse. Kit was always the showrunner. I was just the runner.

Doubt crowded into my head, and I tried to push every negative thought from consuming me. There was a system I used—some meditation, some affirmations that had helped me free myself from the shit my crappy foster families had tried to keep me in my entire childhood. Ms. Mixen had been the only decent one among them, and it was that sweet old hippie lady who had taught me to channel my energy, to focus when the shit of my life threatened to overwhelm me. Like it was now.

"Woman up," I told myself, turning to face Johnny's desk to place my palms flat against the surface. I took in a breath, pulling in all the thoughts that I knew would settle me—*you are strong, you are smart, you are talented*. I exhaled out all the bullshit and negativity that felt like it had a vise grip on my chest—*Dale and Trudy, Dale not saying he loves me, Dale being shot, Dale forgetting absolutely everything that happened between us, Dale touching me like I wanted and never telling me what he felt, Dale...Dale...Dale...*

"Fuck!"

Dropping my head to the desk, I let loose all the stupid frustration. All the loss. All the ridiculous waiting. My weakness waiting for him, wanting him... and I just let myself cry. I didn't know how long I sat there sobbing and feeling completely useless, but after a while, the tears lessened and the tension in my body uncoiled.

"Bella?" I heard, jerking up, mortified when I spotted Johnny staring down at me. His features were tight, eyebrows pushed together, his purple jaw set and clenched as he watched me. "What happened? What the fuck did that motherfucker—"

"No." I stopped him, taking his hand when he knelt beside me. "Please...I'm just feeling...*ah*." I wiped my face with Johnny's handkerchief when he offered it to me. "My friend Madison would say I'm just in my feelings. And I guess I am."

Johnny considered me, pushing back the hair from my face that had stuck all over my forehead and cheeks as I sobbed like a crazy woman against his fancy wooden desk. For a dangerous mafia guy, this man was so affectionate and sweet.

Bet baby sharks are too, I reminded myself. *Until they bite.*

"I...I'm feeling sorry for myself and trying hard not to." Another swipe to dry my face and I forced a smile over my mouth.

Johnny didn't buy it. His expression didn't change, his features sticking in that frozen worry. "What did he do?"

My chin wobbled, and I tried to stop it. I felt ridiculous for acting like such an idiot in front of my boss, but I couldn't control my own body. The tears collected again, hung in my lashes, and when Johnny opened his arms, letting me fall against his chest, I didn't try to keep myself together. Sometimes you just needed a good cry.

"Come," he finally said when my crying had quieted. "Let me take you away from here. We'll start our date early."

I stiffened at the angles and ideas Johnny Carelli might be having. To him, I was sure I looked like a weak, vulnerable woman.

But then he patted my back, pushing my chin up so I could look at him. "My hand to God, I have no angles today, *bella*." He brushed a thumb over my cheek. "I'm just useless at seeing a woman cry. Come, let's see what your friend Johnny can do to make it better."

Chapter Fifteen
Gin

Così Buono was a fine dining Italian restaurant owned by Sofia, a friend of Johnny's cousin Antonia. He had no stake in the place, but he was friendly enough with Sofia to get a private table in a secluded section of the restaurant whenever he asked for one.

"Sofia makes the best *vongole*. Freshest clams in the city."

"And wine?" I was in the mood, and the question made Johnny laugh.

"Yes, *bella*. So much wine you could swim in it." We walked through the door, Johnny nodding to the maître d'. "Michael," Johnny greeted the man, shaking his hand.

Michael smiled as he discreetly slipped the bill Johnny gave him into his jacket pocket.

"Mr. Carelli, Thom will bring you and your guest to the back rooms." He waved over a boy, tall but fit with a pale complexion who seemed completely unbothered by the way the maître d' summoned him with a snap of his fingers.

"The back rooms, Michael?" Johnny said, looking to the right. There was an empty room next to the entrance fitting only three tables. None of which were occupied. From the way Johnny gazed at the corner table situated next to the fireplace, I got the impression that's where he wanted to be. "We'll sit here, next to the fire."

"Ah." The man's eyes shifted toward the seating chart in front of him. He was calm, but something in his composure fractured when Johnny's friendly smile lowered. "Would you not be more comfortable, have more privacy, in the back rooms? Please, I'll show you myself." He walked to the side, grabbing two menus, then froze, his back straightening when Johnny touched his shoulder.

"The fireplace, Michael. I insist." He didn't wait for the man to lead us into the room, and I understood why. The shift in Johnny's tone, the way he touched the maître d's shoulder, so simple, so casual, held a silent threat you'd only notice if you'd spent any time with Johnny Carelli.

He was always friendly, always generous, always pleasant.

Until he wasn't.

"Is there a problem?" I adjusted the napkin in my lap after we sat and the server placed it there, then hurried away from our table.

Johnny leaned on his elbow, fist covering his mouth as he watched the room. His gaze shifted around us to the empty tables immediately at our right, back through the glass door that offered a glimpse into the lobby and entrance. When I tilted my head, expecting an answer, Johnny flicked his fingers, as if to keep me quiet.

"Shouldn't we go…"

"No, *bella,*" he said behind his curled hand, pulling out his phone. He didn't look at the screen as he selected the name he'd chosen from the list and brought the cell to his ear. "Inside." He hung up and placed the phone back in his pocket. Not once letting his attention leave the rooms that surrounded us.

"Johnny," I said, my stomach knotting as a thousand scenarios of danger and fear overtook the depression I'd felt just an hour before in Johnny's office. Fear overtook sadness. Trumped it every time, and right then, I'd trade a weak, sobbing Gin Sullivan for the one sitting in the middle of some unknown threat with an actual mafia prince.

When I curled my napkin in my hand, head turning to get a look over my shoulder, Johnny stopped me, reaching across the table to grab my fingers. "We're fine," he said with a soft expression, but still tense. "Nothing will happen to you, I promise."

"Why am I not convinced?"

The question seemed to surprise him just enough for Johnny to shift his focus from whatever was happening outside that glass door to me. His smile was easy then, but it didn't last long. "My *bella*, I'd never let anyone touch a hair on that beautiful red head."

Behind me, the noise of the lobby grew louder as the door opened. Johnny dropped my hand, and a brief, cautious smile moved back over his mouth as a woman approached the table.

"Sofia." He stood to reach down and kiss both her cheeks. "So good to see you."

The woman he kissed was tall, looked to be in her late thirties. She had a pleasant smile, and a cropped, blond pixie cut surrounded her angular face. She wore a chef's jacket, pristine and starched, and had to lift up on her toes to receive his kiss. "Johnny. Ugh, still so freaking handsome." She stepped back, squeezing his hand as she moved in front of him. "You're so stubborn. Gave poor Michael a fit," she told him, glancing down at me, her smile warm, friendly. "And who's this?"

"Michael was insistent. I wonder why," he answered, navigating Sofia to his side as he waved at me. "This is Gin Sullivan. We're working on a...project together. I'm expanding into television."

"Television?" She extended a hand to me and stepped right in front of Johnny as she did. It was a weird little dance they were doing, but obvious, even to me.

And when I stood and took Sofia's hand, one glance at Johnny's face told me I wasn't wrong in assuming something was happening that he didn't like.

"Well," Sofia said, grabbing my hand in a friendly double grip. "It's so nice to meet you, Gin. Please, enjoy your meal. Anything you like, it's on me. I recommend the *vongole...*"

"That's what Johnny suggested." My attention shifted back to the man in question as he stood calmly, not watching us, gaze back on the rooms around us.

"Did he?" Sofia asked and gave his arm a squeeze. "Oh, you're always bragging on my—"

"Sofia, cut the shit." Johnny's eyes were sharper now. His tone deepened and lowered enough that I heard the threat between each syllable.

"Johnny..." Sofia tried, dropping her hands from his arms. She attempted a weak smile. Even forced out a faint laugh, but it did little to convince anyone that she was amused.

"What are you hiding?" He focused on her face, his attention sharp and guarded. He was beautiful. So powerful. So strong. But it was the first time I'd seen how menacing Johnny Carelli could be.

Sofia took a step back. She didn't look scared, but I didn't figure she was stupid. There was a boundary she was crossing. I could make that out in how she didn't yell at him and kick him out of her business. She might own it, she might run it, but something about Johnny and the way he carried himself announced with very little effort that you didn't treat him with the same casual bluntness that most bossy customers got. If Sofia knew Johnny's cousin, she knew who and what he was, and that knowledge was what had the woman looking on guard.

"I'm not hiding anything, Johnny. It's not like that..."

He took a step closer to her with his gaze still focused on her face, one hand in his pocket like he wasn't worried or irritated that something was happening he had no control over. "Then why don't you tell me what it's like, *cara?*"

Sofia pressed her lips together as though she had to force back the words beating to escape her closed mouth. Johnny lifted a hand to brush a fallen strand of hair from her shoulder before he rested his palm there.

"I-I..." Sofia stuttered. Her expression shifted into a wince when Johnny squeezed her shoulder. I thought he might be hurting her and was about to beg him to stop, but his gaze had left her face. His entire focus, in fact, was outside the door and on the woman staring at him through the glass.

"Dio mio." The words rushed out in an awed, amazed sound.

"Johnny, please don't..." Sofia tried, going silent when he shook his head and held his hand in front of her face to quiet her.

The man's eyes went wide. His mouth dropped open, and all semblance of calm seemed to leave

Johnny as he walked around Sofia. He met the woman as she walked through the door and stood just two feet in front of him in the center of the room.

I'd never seen her equal. To say she was beautiful seemed like some stupid, pathetic description that couldn't come close to doing her justice. She was striking and looked like she'd stepped right out of the pages of *Vogue*, sporting a high-waisted black pencil skirt and a black turtleneck sweater with a beige pea coat hanging from her shoulders.

She was radiant, timeless, with dark olive skin and wavy black hair, a perfectly oval face, and sharp, exaggerated cheekbones. Her chin was square and strong but feminine. Her long, straight nose was tipped at the end, and her mouth was full, the bottom lip only a fraction larger than the voluminous top. But it was her eyes, those enormous green eyes, lit with a quiet fury that stood out among all that elegant perfection, and they were focused like lasers on Johnny.

"Merda," he said, finally finding his voice. He came closer, and the movement seemed to wake something inside her.

The amazed expression on her face shifted, transformed into something that reminded me of a tiger ready to pounce.

"Sammy…"

Those beautiful eyes narrowed, her full, pouting top lip curled, and the woman shook her head. "No." She reached back to slap Johnny Carelli, that fearsome mafia prince, so hard across the face that he stumbled back.

"Son of a bitch." Sofia followed after Sammy as she turned on her heel to leave.

"Johnny?" I said.

He only stood there, holding his face. He wore an expression that alternated between disbelief, shock, and outright joy, as though he felt so many things and none of them made sense to him.

"You okay?"

It took several seconds for him to refocus, for him to drop the astounded, awed expression. When he did, it was like a fuse had been lit inside him. "Forgive me." He did not bother to look back at me as he hurried through the door and after the woman who clearly had Johnny under her spell.

Chapter Sixteen
Gin

"So, something happened today."

"Something?" Cara's voice was a little pleased and mildly curious. I had a sneaking suspicion that pregnancy and being idle had bored the woman. She seemed too eager for gossip.

"Well, yeah. It was weird, actually." I relaxed against the club chair next to the window in my hotel room with my feet propped up on the arm. "Johnny took me to Così Buono today for lunch."

"Oh, Sofia's place. *Dio mio,* I'd kill for her chicken piccata. So good."

"Anyway..." I continued, ignoring the low moan Cara made. I remembered when Madison's sister stayed with her while she was pregnant. The mere mention of certain food would have the woman turning into a moaning, drooling mess. "So Sofia seemed to be trying to keep someone away from Johnny, and he knew it."

Cara went quiet on the other end of the phone. I could only make out the distant muffle of Kiel's voice as he sang in the background, and then Cara moved, calling out something to her husband before her feet sounded on a floor and a door closed and then there was silence.

"Was it...Sammy?"

I sat up, dropping my feet to the floor. "Oh God, how did you know?"

"Ah...*merda*. Look, Gin, I should have warned you about this. I didn't think he'd be stupid enough to bring you to Sofia's place..."

"Why not?" Holding the phone away from my ear, I put it on the table and hit the speaker button.

"Because Sofia and Sammy were at St. Mary's together. It's how Johnny knows her."

"He said your cousin Antonia was Sofia's friend."

"She is. They were all at St. Mary's together. He's fine bringing his boys there, that's not the problem, but he knows...Ugh. He's just never brought a woman there. Even though there's nothing between you, it sends a message. Christ, I wish I had a drink." She cleared her throat, fingers tapping against something as I waited for her to continue. "Okay, tell me everything that happened. Every detail."

And I did, rehashing the strange behavior of the maître d' and how Johnny seemed to be aware the man was trying to hide something. How Sofia tried to block Johnny's view of the doorway and then...Sammy's arrival.

"And then she just stared at him as he gawked at her. Her lip curled and her hand shook, and I swear to God, the woman reared back and slapped him hard across the face."

"Oh *Dio!*"

"Well, she did seem mad enough to..."

"No, not her. God bless her, Sammy has every right to smack my stupid brother around. *Merda*...what did he do when she slapped him?"

"Went after her."

"He left you alone?"

"He did. Cara, who is Sammy?"

"Ah, Gin...that's a long, sad story, and my *chooch* of a brother doesn't come off very well in it. It's also not my secret." She groaned, and I heard Kiel muttering something to her about a back massage. "I will say that if all Sammy did was smack him, then it's an improvement. There was a time when she promised to kill him if she ever saw him again."

"She sounds like a tough woman."

"That's the thing," Cara said, stifling another satisfied moan. "Before she met Johnny, she wasn't. She was sweet, kind, and very chaste. Had plans to stay that way, and well...things happened." Kiel said something to her, and Cara muttered back before she returned to our conversation. "My brother isn't proud of what he did to Sammy. In fact, he's told me many times it's the worst thing he's ever done in his life and he never expects to be forgiven. But deep down, Gin, he has a good heart."

"I hear you," I said, distracted by the memory of another good man who once told me the same thing about himself. "Thanks, Cara. You take care of yourself."

"You too. And don't feel too bad for my brother. He can take care of himself."

We said our goodbyes, and I opened my text messages, noticing that Dale had only sent one, and that was early this morning.

Words always get in the way.

They did. Somehow, it was the words we didn't say that injured the most. It was the silence that kept us from what we want.

Johnny had done a lot of bad in his life. To hear him tell it, so had Dale, both for very different reasons. I had no idea what Johnny's were, but I knew that the things Dale did were because he thought it would bring honor to himself or his country. There was a difference between those two men, but neither one of them believed their sins could be forgiven.

Always figured I'd sinned too much, did too many dirty things to ever be forgiven, he'd once told me.

For a long time, I didn't believe that.

For a long time, I didn't think there was a thing Dale could do that would stop me from loving him or always wanting him. He'd pushed me away before. He'd broken the camel's back.

The last time was just a week before I left Seattle for Portland and Trudy had shown up on set. It had been his first week back, and I'd managed to avoid him at all costs. Kit and Kane seemed fine with me using Asher as our go-between, but that wouldn't last forever. Dale had cornered me to tell me as much.

"Next time you need something from me, you come ask me," he'd said, looking pissed that I'd sent Asher to fetch Dale's lunch order instead of asking him myself like I'd done every day for two years.

"The lunch request is for anyone who doesn't eat craft services. Asher takes those special orders now." I didn't bother looking up from my laptop as he hovered over my desk.

"Since when?"

"Since I damn well don't want to do it!"

We stared at each other. Both of us glaring. Both looking half crazed and fully out of control when Asher walked into the trailer.

"Dale?"

"What?" Dale yelled.

"You got a visitor. She...she says she's your wife."

I laughed, utterly unamused as I sat back down, ignoring him when he let out a curse and stomped to the door. The kid didn't follow, watching Dale as he left.

"Asher, shut the door please, and get back to work." *My fingertips ached from how hard I punched on the keyboard.*

"Yes, ma'am, but I was actually coming in here for you too." *He came back in, closing the door behind him.* "The delivery guy is here with that shipment of flooring, but it doesn't look right. And he says he's already unloaded it and won't load it back. Kane and Kit are out to lunch, I don't know where Bill is, and Dale is...well..."

"For heaven's sake... Okay." *I moved away from the desk and followed Asher out to the large truck and two skinny assholes sitting on top of my shipment of scraped walnut flooring, drinking sodas, and flicking cigarette ashes on the fresh gravel driveway. They looked unbothered that they were pissing me off just by half-assing their work.* "Get up and open that box!"

It took a good twenty minutes to straighten out the order and send those lazy jerks back to their warehouse—with the flooring reloaded in their truck. By the time I finished yelling at them, I felt better. It helped having an outlet for my anger, especially when they deserved it for only phoning in their jobs.

My good mood didn't last. In fact, it got infinitely worse when I headed back to the trailer and overheard Dale's raised voice and Trudy's loud shriek just ten feet away from the back of our makeshift office.

"You are out of your fucking mind if you think I would ever even consider taking you back!"

"Baby, you don't mean that. I know you don't. We were so good together—"

"Until you started fucking around!"

I should have moved. I took steps, four of them, but stopped abruptly when that foul thing pulled me into the middle of her drama.

"You were already running around with that red-headed whore. Don't deny it. I see the way she looks at you. I know how you've always looked at her."

"First off," Dale said, his tone getting thicker, deeper, as though he was going to make her understand. "I ever hear you refer to my friend as a whore again, I swear to Christ, everyone at your hospital will find out about the company that daddy of yours runs and the bribes he pays to the doctors at your hospital to get the doses increased for their patients. Pharmaceutical companies bribing doctors so they can sell more drugs is against the damn law. I'm guessing your bosses and their bosses would love to know how you introduced your daddy and your friends, or how just two weeks after you left me, you were already living with that pain management specialist they just hired. The one who got in a whole heap of trouble in Dallas for exchanging lap dances for opioid scrips. Yeah, bet your ass didn't think I knew about that shit." When he spoke again, there was a laugh in his tone that unsettled me. "I was a SEAL for twelve years, Trudy. You think I can't find out shit people don't want known?

"Second, and you might want to get this straight in your head. Might save the next sucker you manage to convince you're worth the trouble having. Not every person on this planet fucks around on the people they claim to love. That's just how you think the world goes. And third, and most important of all, it is none of your fucking business how I look at Gin or any other woman in the world. Doesn't matter anyway. You fucked that for me. You fucked me over so hard. You made me distrust everything I thought I knew about people who are good or decent. I can't ever bring myself to love anyone else again, you rotten bitch. There. You happy now? You ready to pretend you didn't fucking destroy me? You still wanna play like we can have a normal, happy life again? No? Good. Me the fuck either."

I should have gotten my ass in gear and pretended I didn't hear a damn bit of that admission. But I didn't, and every word felt like a knife in the gut.

"I can't ever bring myself to love anyone else again."

Right then, that's when I knew. It had to be the reason he pretended what happened between us at the cabin had never actually happened at all. Dale wished it hadn't. He couldn't love me or anyone else.

I felt stupid just standing there. My stomach knotted up and coiled like a spring, hurting so badly, I had to hold my palm flat against my belly just to keep it settled. That was how Dale found me, stepping out from behind the trailer, his gaze shooting straight to my face, to what I guessed was a mix of horror and disappointment with the tears that had started to build up in my eyes.

"Shit." I heard him say, walking toward me with his hand held up. He stopped when I shook my head.

"Nuh-uh." I turned on my heel to get as far away from him as quickly as I could.

"Gin, hold up!" He ran behind me.

I made it to my truck, cranking it and throwing it into reverse before Dale had cleared the golf carts circled around the back of the set.

"Will you stop?" I heard him, but I kept going, wanting nothing more than to put distance, as much of it as I could, between us. I parked in the back of Madison's gated lot hidden behind her privacy fence. I stayed on her sofa because I knew Dale would come looking for me. He hadn't stopped trying to talk to me for weeks since the shooting. I just hadn't wanted to hear what he had to say. Now, hearing what he believed, I realized with a grief I thought might topple me, it would make no difference what he said. It would never be what I wanted to hear from him.

I'd toyed with the idea of a transfer. There was another show filming in Portland, one about rehabbing old homes. Portland had those in abundance. But it was right there on Maddy's sofa that I sent out the request, texting Kit to have Bill rush it through.

Three nights later, with the weekend done and having taken a personal day, I was still camped out *on Maddy's sofa. I was avoiding life, avoiding the incessant texting from Dale and his frequent drop-bys at my house with him stopping in my driveway next door. That Monday night, on Madison's sofa, checking my email while she binged* Scandal *for the fourth time, I got the response I'd been waiting for.*

Good news, Ms. Sullivan, *the email read.* Your transfer has been approved, and you can report to the set of "Make Me Pretty Again" in two weeks.

That was plenty of time for me to find a place to rent and get gone.

"Maddy?" I said, talking over Olivia shaming Fitz because he always *deserved it. She nodded, too engrossed to answer me. "Your brother still have that moving company?"*

"Yeah." She paused the screen to watch me. "Why?"

"Think I'm gonna hire him."

A week later, I sat in my Armada, watching the moving truck pull down the road with everything I owned in the back of it. I was ready to leave Seattle and all the heartbreak in it behind.

"You sure about this?" Kit asked, and I could make out the sniffle in her tone through the phone.

"I have to." I looked one last time at my empty bungalow, wiping my face dry as I pulled onto the road. "I'll never get any peace if I don't."

"Um...Dale...he's been calling and calling. Keeps pestering Kane and everyone on set, wanting to know where you are."

He would. I'd gotten more messages from him. A dozen, at least. Until, finally, he agreed to give me some breathing room. But that had been nearly five days ago. I'd changed my number after the second day.

"Give him some time." I blinked quickly when more tears collected in my eyes. "He'll get over it soon enough."

"You sure about..."

"Shit, he's here."

"What?" Kit asked.

"I... Let me call you back."

"You better."

I pulled to the side of the road, parallel parking two houses down from my bungalow. I watched as Dale ran up my drive, jumping onto my front porch to bang on my door. He didn't wait for an answer. He kept up a constant barrage of pounding, then moved to the front window, cupping his hands around his eyes as he peeked inside.

"Walk away," I whispered, knowing it was best.

All this was for the best.

After he waited a good ten minutes, his fist pounding against the siding above the window, Dale finally sat down on the front porch. His feet dangled off the side as he slumped against one of the columns.

I knew this man. I knew what every expression meant. I knew what he thought when he scowled. What he felt when he curled his fist, ready to slam it into a wall. Just then, Dale tore off his New Orleans Saints ball cap, scrubbing his face as he leaned against his knees like he couldn't quite figure out what his next step would be.

Then, like a wild man, the fool jumped up and kicked the door in. He tore through my empty house, screaming for me. My name so loud, I heard it two houses down.

"I can't ever bring myself to love anyone else again."

I didn't stop the tears when they came this time. I didn't stop the low, deep, aching sobs when they left my throat.

"Walk away," I told him, looking at the man I loved in my rearview mirror as I pulled back onto the road, doing that very thing myself.

Chapter Seventeen
Dale

Turns out, *I fucking hate New York.*

The city was nice enough, the people were friendly, but the traffic sucked. The noise was unbearable, and I needed to see the mountains or the ocean or a trail that wasn't surrounded by concrete. I'd spent most of my adult life with no home to speak of, and somehow, I found myself missing Seattle because it was the closest thing to home I'd ever had.

Even though Gin wouldn't be there when I got back.

I dodged two yellow cabs as I moved through the intersection, following Joe's directions as best as I could when the man told me where I could find Carelli.

"You better not go in there trying to whoop that man's ass again," he'd told me, smoking a cigarette at the bus stop next to the building where the show had been set up. "Those motherfuckers have guns and know how to hide the bodies."

"I ain't a Girl Scout. I just need a quick word, and I'll be off." I let the words hang there, not bothering to elaborate.

Joe had looked me over, abandoning his cigarette. If I wasn't wrong, he looked disappointed in me, and he didn't even know shit about me. Usually took a month or two before I started pissing folks off enough to disappoint them.

"You just gonna let him have her? No fight or nothing?"

"I clocked him," I said, and I knew the defense was weak the second it was out of my mouth.

"And?"

"It's complicated."

That made the man cackle, slapping my shoulder as he leaned against the light pole next to the bus stop. "No, shit. Women usually are." He'd told me where to go, how to get there, and gave me a warning—don't fuck with anyone in that bar. They *all* know *people*.

I didn't much care about that. I could handle myself if I needed to, but hell, Carelli's *people* had once fucked Kiel up so bad he almost didn't make it back home to Seattle in one piece. And Kiel was a big motherfucker.

I shook off the worry, looking at the intersection, when I spotted Carelli's bodyguard leaning against a stretch limo, bouncing a ball on the sidewalk next to a sign that read Demonte's. He'd spot me if I just walked right by him, likely would clock me for getting past him on the set and wailing on his boss. I didn't have time for that shit and didn't want to end up in a New York City jail or at the bottom of a river somewhere.

I waited and watched the crowd, spotting the trickle of foot traffic increasing as the afternoon got later and later. I would have to reschedule my flight, but then, maybe that was a good thing. I had no expectations of seeing Gin. I'd burned that bridge. She left. I'd let her go. Trudy had come to New York to get me home, and now I knew why. It wasn't some bullshit excuse. I was needed and not by her. I'd go, but I had to make sure Gin would be looked after. Even if Carelli was a piece of shit criminal, he would protect her. I knew that much. Hated to ask him, but for her, I'd do anything. Even beg a favor of a mafia asshole.

I saw my chance and followed behind a group of guys heading off of a bus and walking toward the front entrance. From the looks of the place, it didn't strike me as a spot Carelli would find suitable. He was a little prissy for a roughneck bar. But Joe swore this was where he'd be because this was where most of the crew hung out. Where Carelli found most of the guys he'd hire for odd jobs and day labor. Where he'd found Joe, in fact, so I took the man's word for it.

I fell behind four guys taller than me, sporting jeans and Carhartt jackets as they headed for the door. I slipped between them when the tallest opened the door. He nodded me in, and I dipped my chin in thanks, my eyes adjusting to the darkened bar as I moved inside.

It was mostly empty except for the front left side of the bar. Off to the right was a second area with around ten tables. In the center of the room was a second level, with a small set of stairs leading up into another bar area.

There were waitresses maneuvering around the larger area. They were checking on the small crowds gathered and refilling pitchers of beer or serving shots. But most of the activity was happening at the bar. It was there I slipped onto a stool, nodding to the old man behind the counter when he asked for my order.

"Jack. Straight."

"You want a tab?" I shook my head, and he turned away from me to pour the glass.

The old man took the ten I left on the bar and then walked away, leaving me to study my surroundings in the long antique mirror that hung over the bar. There were no TVs in the place, but a vintage jukebox was at the center in the back and played an old Al Martino song. I looked around, my attention on that mirror, watching, squinting close when I made out the couple in the back of the bar next to one of the columns.

Gin and Johnny.

He leaned heavily on the table, balled fist at his temple as she sat cross-legged, not touching him, her body turned in his direction. Something had clearly happened, something that had put that worried expression on her face. Something that made Carelli down two shots of tequila before Gin took the bottle from him.

Couldn't help myself. Didn't see a need to.

I moved the long way around the bar, bypassing the center area. I looped up the stairs, coming to the right of the upper-level bar to slip in an empty booth just above where Johnny and Gin sat. There were thin slates between the columned wall, and I could just make out the worry on Gin's face as she listened to Johnny speak. The music was louder in this part of the bar and had switched to a faster Dean Martin tune. I could only catch a few words from either of them.

"What...say..." I made out from Gin, frowning as Carelli pushed off the table, running his fingers through his hair. Then she nodded, and whatever that asshole told her had her touching his wrist, squeezing it.

I thought she'd let go. That was just my Gingerbread being kind to a friend, but then Carelli put his hand over hers and kissed her knuckles. My stomach dropped like I'd been gut-punched when I caught the blush that brightened her face.

"Come on, baby. Don't buy his shit," I whispered, willing her to hear me. Willing that asshole to get his hands away from her.

I'd socked him once. I'd do it again, but with one glance around this place, to the pictures on the walls—Carelli and Cara in a few of them, their father in many—and the guys I'd spotted from the crew, I understood I'd be outmanned. It would be stupid to try to level any kind of attack when this was clearly a solo mission.

"Sammy." I heard Carelli say, and his head dropped again. This time, he kept it down, and I watched Gin's face. All that sweetness, all that beauty always there, ready to be given away whenever she wanted, shifting as that asshole cried, leaning forward so she could cradle him against her chest.

"Motherfucker."

Gin touched his back, giving him her sweet comfort. She gave him her softness that I'd had so many times. I'd fucked up royally, but Carelli didn't squander it. He took what she gave him like he needed it. Like he didn't need anything else. Killed me to do it, but I watched them. I watched as Carelli went on crying, holding on to Gin, as she kissed his forehead. Her lips moved, and she said things to him that probably felt good, that probably eased him. Had to. She'd done it for me a dozen times or more when I'd fucked myself, over and over again.

I couldn't look away as Carelli straightened, as he thanked her. He kept his fucking hands on her soft face as he kept his eyes closed. Then he pulled her mouth to his and took her kiss. From *my* Gin.

She was going to push him away. I knew it. How could she not? Gin couldn't take that touch. She wouldn't let him cry and kiss her and think it was real? Not when I'd just been inside her. Not when she'd spent years waiting—

But I hadn't given her what she wanted. I hadn't done a damn thing but stew in my own fucking misery while my best friend got over me.

Gin didn't pull away from Carelli. She didn't stop him.

My Gingerbread took his kiss and let him pull her close. She let that man hold her and take her mouth like she'd forgotten that I'd been there first.

That I wanted to be there again and again.

Forever.

There was only so much a man could take.

This was on me. I'd let her walk away. I hadn't tried to explain a fucking thing.

This was my fault.

But I damn well didn't have to watch it.

So, I didn't. I didn't watch, and I didn't look back as I walked away.

Chapter Eighteen
Gin

What was I doing? No...this wasn't. I couldn't.

"Johnny, no," I said, pulling away from his kiss.

I hated the look he gave me. Half relief, half disappointment. We were both so damn mixed up by the people we wanted. The people who didn't want us back.

"*Bella*..." His voice was gravelly, rough, but the apology was sincere.

"It's okay," I said, squeezing his hand. "I promise. It's fine."

The place was dark and nearly empty except for the loud men at the bar in the front and the waitress who kept coming by to check if Johnny had enough tequila.

From the way he'd tasted, he'd had enough.

God. *Tasted*. Johnny Carelli kissed me.

He'd been upset and wouldn't elaborate other than to say that Sammy had eviscerated him out on the sidewalk next to Sofia's restaurant.

"She looked at me like I was the lowest filth...like she's never..."

"You still love her." It wasn't a question.

I was familiar with unrequited love, and Johnny didn't deny it.

We understood each other better now.

At least we could relate to each other.

"Bella," he repeated, voice aching and low. "I'm... *Dio,* I'm sorry."

"Johnny..."

He lifted up my chin, and his gaze moved over my face. "I was...upset, and you were very kind. I got... away from myself."

I spotted the question in his eyes before he asked it. Johnny wanted to know if I was repulsed or turned on by his touch.

He wanted to know, like me, if there was something between us worth exploring.

I was confused, but I wasn't stupid.

"We're both in a rotten place, aren't we? Both so mixed up."

His smile was slow to come and sweet. It remained there as Johnny wiped his face and mouth dry. *"Tesoro...*I cannot promise you anything but friendship."

I sat back, leaning one elbow on the arm of my chair. "I think I'm starting to realize I could use a good friend right about now."

He moved forward again, resting his hand on my arm. The feel of it was comforting and warm. "There are no guarantees in this life, and love, well, that is not for everyone."

"No," I said, meaning it. "It's not."

"But friendship...that, *bella*, is for always."

"It can be, yes," I said, pushing down the small flame of bitterness I felt. Dale had once been my friend. Sometimes I wished he would have stayed my friend and only my friend.

"So, I am sad over the bad things I did to Sammy..." Johnny moved his chair forward, rubbing his fingers along my arm. "And you are sad that Hunter can't seem to get himself together enough to keep you happy."

I didn't disagree with that assessment either, but wouldn't fill Johnny in on why Dale couldn't make me happy. Whatever was happening with Trudy and the baby, it seemed to me Dale had made a choice, and I wasn't it.

Johnny opened his hand, offering it to me. It only took me a second to take it. "What if we promise to remain friends, only friends and just have fun? No sex, no kissing or anything else other than a good time, hard work, and more fun celebrating our eventual success?"

"That sounds perfect, Mr. Carelli."

"Bene." He lifted my hand to his mouth. The kiss he placed there was soft, sweet, and made me feel something I hadn't in a long time—happy.

Chapter Nineteen

Gin

Three weeks later- Seattle

Some things fit.

Peanut butter and chocolate.

Lavender on a pillow.

Strawberries and champagne.

Jazz on a Saturday night in a smoky club.

Sometimes things are perfect, and you know it. It's instinctual. You can see how perfectly the fitting happens in one glance. I saw that well enough watching Cara and Kiel hold their three-week-old son.

They fit, the pair of them, almost better than anyone I knew. Four hours in a hospital with nurses and doctors moving around them, and then there was no "pair of them" anymore. There was someone new. Someone precious, and just like that, Cara and Kiel were a family.

It fit them.

"My heart," Mr. Carelli said, his frail smile growing.

Cara held her son next to her father's chest so the old man could get a better look at his first grandchild.

"*Dio mio, il mio amore prezioso*. He is perfect. Like his *mama*. Like his *nonna* Theresa, God rest." He leaned forward to kiss the baby, his smile wide, expression amazed. "*Bene. Molto buona.*"

"Thank you, *papa*." Cara choked on her words as Kiel stood next to her. His eagle eyes were on his wife and son, sometimes shifting around Kane and Kit's large home, to the bodyguards Johnny had insisted follow us when we left New York for Seattle to meet the newest addition to the Carelli clan.

"Now," the old man said, his gaze following the baby when he began to fuss and Cara stood to pace near her father's wheelchair to jostle the baby asleep. "The christening...in New York. St. Matthew's, of course..."

Kiel's features were tense at the mention of returning to the city with his family. So was his mother, Mrs. Kaino, as she stood next to him. Both seemed reassured when Old Man Carelli began discussing the plans he had for the baby's christening and the security he'd provide for everyone.

"My entire security team and Johnny...*figlio*... come..."

The old man called Johnny to his side, and he patted my back as a way to excuse himself as he joined his father. I didn't mind. I'd become accustomed to dismissals whenever the elder Carelli needed Johnny over the past three weeks. The show kept me busy, so did plans for what might come next, and when it didn't, Johnny made time for me.

It was nice, being around him. Having no pressure at all beyond what meals we ate and what shows we took in on the weekends. There were a few concerts and some dinners with his friends. It was fun. It was friendship. It was all...very...nice.

But it wasn't hikes up Mt. Rainier or Clint Eastwood movies on a Sunday night. It wasn't drive-in movies in Tacoma or picnics with Kit at whatever new flea market she discovered, dragging Kane and Dale along to lift heavy furniture she'd stuff in her storage building for a later show. It wasn't moonlight beer guzzling in an open field with my best friend talking about life or talking about nothing at all.

It wasn't family, the family I'd made in Seattle.

New York and Johnny and the life I'd started to make there was nice.

But it wasn't home.

It wasn't family.

I shook myself from the haze of thought I fell into as Johnny slipped to his father's side, and I used his departure as an excuse to catch my breath and track down Kit.

It had been a week at least since I'd heard from her. Mainly because they were prepping for a new shoot. This one on the lake again, more secluded since Kit's show had drawn a wider audience and been assigned an earlier time slot. They were pulling out all the stops. The prep required a lot more work than they'd ever had to put into the show before. At least, that's what Kit mentioned the last time I'd spoken to her. When I'd called to find out if Dale had come back to Seattle.

He had. Kit couldn't give me any more details than that. It had been the first time since I'd known her that my friend appeared to take a side in the Gin/Dale fiasco, and I hadn't been her choice. That stung more than I thought it would.

I rounded the back of the den, following the sound of laughter I heard in the kitchen. My stomach tightened when I heard Kane's booming chuckle and Kit's teasing tone.

"Stop it, you'll ruin it." She slapped his hand away from the pan of roasted salmon she was bent over in the open oven. "Your mother will kill you if you mess up this salmon. She's been working on it all afternoon."

"She won't know." Kane pinched off a corner before she could stop him. "She's too busy fussing over her grandson."

"And hinting for more," Kit muttered, pushing the dish back into the oven before she closed it.

"Oh? Well, we can remedy that right now..." He grabbed Kit around the waist, hoisting her up onto the countertop quickly enough that she released a high-pitched squeal of laughter before she looked over his shoulder and spotted me.

"Stop. Gin!" She looked surprised and mildly relieved that I'd interrupted them. A small family get-together celebrating the birth of the latest addition didn't strike me as the right place to start on the next branch of the Kaino family tree.

"Am I interrupting?" I asked, fiddling with the toothpick still in my hand from the cheese wedge I'd grabbed as I'd passed a platter in the den. "I can disappear..."

Kane stepped away from his wife. "Yeah. That much we know."

I'd expected his attitude. Kane was Dale's friend. It had never seemed to sit well with him, the way I'd left Seattle without any real goodbyes to anyone, especially my former best friend. With Dale returning to Seattle alone, my imagination could fill in the blanks for what he'd told everyone about his trip to New York and why I'd stayed.

"Kane." Kit jabbed him in the ribs. "Be nice." She pushed her husband aside and greeted me, arms wide to wrap me in a tight hug. "Oh, Gin. I'm so happy you made it." Relief flooded me as I relaxed into her embrace, realizing I might have made too many assumptions about what side Kit had chosen.

She kept her hands on my arms then looked me over, attention on my face. "You look amazing."

"You too, honey."

She looked happy, the smile on her face wide, making a light brighten her eyes.

I threw a glance to Kane, irritated when he seemed more interested in filling ice in glasses than acknowledging me at all.

Kit followed my gaze, then gave her hand a flippant wave. "Ignore him. His mom has been here all week, and he's grumpy because we haven't…" She stopped speaking when Kane cleared his throat, silencing her explanation before she finished it. "Well," she continued. "We've been spending *most of our time* with her."

"Ah." I tried to stifle my laugh. "Well, Kane, your nephew is beautiful."

He turned then, nodding once before he went back to ignoring me.

"And how's New York? You said you guys landed a meeting?" She smiled when I nodded, clapping her hands. "That's amazing. When is it?"

"In two weeks. Johnny's confident."

That was an understatement. The man was cocky, convinced the network would be falling all over itself to get us under contract.

"And you're not?"

"I…I don't know." I leaned a hip against the counter as Kit poured us each a glass of wine. I took mine when she offered it, downing a good sip before I continued. "I like the crew, and the premise is good."

"But…"

Another sip. This one longer and I set my glass down next to me. "It's not *our* crew. It's not *our* show. You aren't there, Kane isn't…"

The man himself turned, folding his arms over his chest as he rested against the countertop to watch us. When he looked at me, he wasn't frowning, though. He seemed genuinely curious.

"There's something…missing."

"Something." Kit lowered back on her elbows. "Or someone."

I knew we'd come to this. In fact, I'd thought we'd get here a lot sooner, but Kit did what she wanted in her own time. I'd expected nothing less from her.

"Kit," Kane warned, getting utterly ignored by his wife.

"You haven't asked about him, and you've been here, what, half an hour?"

"I was in the den gawking at the baby." I downed even more wine. "Besides, I wasn't sure anyone would tell me anything." When I stared at Kane, the man's expression didn't change, but Kit glanced back at him like it was ridiculous for me to be cautious.

"Dale had to leave." She waved her hand again when Kane grunted. "He didn't want you knowing because he knows how you'd feel about it. He couldn't just let Anthony rot."

I opened my mouth, a complaint of disappointment on the tip of my tongue.

"And before you start making assumptions, I'll tell you right now. Trudy was in the middle of it because

Tony landed in Seattle off a bus from New Orleans already going through withdrawals from the shit he was on. He was half dead when he got here, and Trudy was the nurse on duty in the ER. She was trying to get Dale here because..."

Kane cleared his throat again, and this time, Kit quieted.

She set her glass down and smiled at me. "Well, Jazmine showed up a few days later and knew she wouldn't be able to handle things on her own. Dale... was going to tell you this but he... Well... Before he..." She fidgeted with her glass, not watching me, looking embarrassed and awkward before Kane walked to her side, laying a hand on her shoulder.

"Before he spotted you and Carelli in that bar making out."

"He... I... *What?*"

Kane nodded, not bothering to elaborate.

"That wasn't... Johnny was upset because..."

"So you and Carelli aren't together?" Kane glared at me like he was determined not to believe anything I said.

"It's...no... Not at all. We're just friends. He was upset that day. He kissed me, and I turned him down. It...wasn't a long kiss. "

"Hmm. Dale thought it was long enough, I suppose." Kit lifted her hand to thread her fingers with Kane's on her shoulder. "You love Dale. You love everything about him. Even the stupid shit he does, like helping out his addict brother who is likely to screw him over and over again."

I wasn't heartless. I knew Dale wasn't either. Of course, I understood loyalty. I understood having your people's backs, even though I didn't understand anyone letting themselves be taken advantage of over and over. Least of all Dale. But we'd been friends for so long. All of this, he could have told me. I would have listened...

But I didn't. Oh God, I just...didn't.

With Kit and Kane staring at me, waiting like they expected an explanation that would excuse away my stupidity, I grabbed at the first thing that popped into my head. "It's not so simple..."

"Love rarely is, honey."

I tried again, grappling with all the conversations Dale and I didn't have and should have had when we were together in New York. There'd been so much confusion and not enough honesty. Then I remembered the one sticking point. The baby. Trudy's baby. Could I stomach being with him if he had a baby with Trudy? Was he worth the risk?

Glancing at my friend, I blinked, tightening my grip around the base of my wineglass. "But what about the...baby?"Kane and Kit looked at each other, surprise coloring their faces like they hadn't expected I'd discovered that many of Dale's secrets.

"You know about her?" Kane said.

"I...know."

"She's beautiful," Kit said, her features softening, and something glinted in her eyes. "And sweet."

"And you can't make him choose just because it's not an ideal situation," Kane said, defending his friend. When I glared at him, Kane lifted his hand, a surrender and an apology at once. "Sorry, darlin', but those don't exist anymore."

Some things fit. Kane and Kit. Kiel and Cara, but Dale and me, even Dale and me and this baby? Could we fit?

Man, the thought of it did something to my insides, made them warm and coil tight, a pleasant sensation that did a lot to crack the walls I'd constructed around my heart.

He'd told me once, that night in the cabin, that he'd do anything for me. Maybe he didn't remember it. Maybe everything he'd felt, everything he'd promised, got locked somewhere in the spaces of his mind behind whatever it was war and violence had done to him, whatever Trudy's betrayal had done, and whatever that anesthesia had done. But when he'd spoken those words to me, Dale had meant them.

If I really thought about it, he'd meant them when he held me in that New York hotel room, when he took me over and over again that entire night. When he sang in the shower and couldn't keep the joy out of his off-key tune. He'd meant it all those times, even if he couldn't remember what he'd said to me in the first place.

Then, as Kit and Kane watched me, as all the recollections swam in my head, as I fought to find a glimmer that marked what *I* had said, what *I* had done, I realized I hadn't given him the same. Not once since that night in the cabin. I'd been hurt. I'd been embarrassed, and I hadn't been a good friend to him.

I hadn't listened.

I pushed back the wineglass, throwing the couple in front of me a smile. The rush of energy I felt was tied up in the excitement to see Dale, to finally listen and hear everything he'd wanted to say for over a year. "I think...I have to go."

"Gin! Wait!" Kit called after me as I tore out of the kitchen, her steps falling behind me. I was out of the kitchen and into the den as quickly as I could move around the guests, and Kit got blocked by the crowd and the Carelli guards.

I waved them off, tossing an apology to Cara as I left. I was nearly to the driveway, not knowing how I'd get to Dale or even sure where he was before I heard feet following behind me, then felt a large, firm grip on my arm.

"*Bella*." I heard, stopping just as I reached the edge of the Kaino driveway, Johnny's voice worried.

Damn. I had to say something to the man about where I was going. He was my ride, after all.

"Johnny..." I started, unsure what to say or how to make any sense of what I felt.

He'd been so good to me for a long time. So willing to lend a hand, so eager to see me smile. He was a criminal, but he wasn't a villain.

"Johnny, I'm sorry. I have..."

Johnny watched me, his expression shifting. His gaze moving over me as I shuffled my feet, and then he seemed to understand where I was going and why I wanted to leave so quickly.

He smiled, moving his hand to my face. I wanted to thank him, to tell him I wished we were different. I wanted to say that, if I could, I'd pray for my heart to change, for his as well, for my love to turn and shift so that what I felt would leave me just to make this man happy. Just to give him a smile that would reach his eyes. But I couldn't. Those were prayers I'd never speak.

Johnny shook his head, shrugging as he slipped his hand into his pocket and stared out onto the empty street. "I just hope that redneck understands what a treasure you are."

"Me too."

"And if he doesn't, *bella*," Johnny said, his attention returning to me, "you come back to me, and I promise I'll give you the world."

I nodded, taking his hug when he held me close, grateful for the man and the kindness he'd shown me.

"Angelo will take you to him."

"Thank you," I told Johnny, and I left him standing there in the driveway, not looking back once.

Chapter Twenty

Gin

Dale's place was different from the last time I'd visited. It was set back off the main road and secluded on a private drive a mile down. It was another half mile up the mountain, then up an inclined driveway before you reached a modern-style ranch surrounded by lush trees.

"Ms. Sullivan, you sure about this?" Angelo leaned forward to look through the windshield at the house. "Looks like a tree house, but it's all dark, and look at those..." He pointed to several boxes packed neatly against the front entrance landing. "Might not be home."

Then as we waited, squinting up at Dale's place, the light over the front door switched on.

"It's fine, Angelo, but thanks." I nodded at the light. "Even if that's just a motion sensor light, I know where he keeps the extra key. I'll be okay." I opened the door, sliding from the car, but I stopped before I left, leaning down to look at the man. "I'm sorry I got your boss clocked."

He frowned as though just remembering.

"It wasn't your fault. He's a SEAL."

"I appreciate that, Ms. Sullivan," the big man said, arm stretched out along the back of the seat. "But I'm a Green Beret. No excuse."

I nodded at the man and turned to face Dale's house. I headed across the small bridge elevated above the ravine that ran beneath the house. The small entrance was lit, but there was no activity behind the windows that flanked the wide-paneled wood door.

How many times had I walked right in without knocking? How often had I hung Christmas wreaths or jack-o'-lanterns in this area just to irritate the always holiday-averse Dale? Even though no kids ever came this far off the main road to trick-or-treat?

But now, I'd have to ring the bell. Everything had changed.

There was a tremor in my fingers when I touched the doorbell. I waited and fidgeted with my clothes, brushing back my ponytail free of flyaways, adjusting my jacket, and pulling down my top. All distractions to keep myself from worrying what Dale would say or do once he opened the door and spotted me on the other side. Last he'd seen of me, Johnny and I were kissing.

From what I could make of Kane's attitude, my guess was Dale wasn't overjoyed about that.

The footsteps I heard on the other side of the door weren't rushed. My heart still quickened as they approached, and the closer they came, the faster my pulse raced. And then the door flew open and Dale blinked down at me.

For a second, he had no reaction at all. I had half a suspicion that Kane had called to warn him I'd be on my way. Then Dale moved his eyebrows up and his mouth dropped open before he recovered, and the small whip of surprise on his features shifted to what I could only determine was cool indifference.

Feeling stupid and awkward, I inhaled, releasing a quick, "Hey," before I lost my nerve.

He didn't answer, but he nodded once, pressing his lips together as he looked me over. He went on watching me, glancing over my shoulder so often that I followed his gaze, then looked back at him, figuring he was likely expecting to see Johnny.

I wanted to avoid the topic of him as long as possible, so I stepped forward, leaning on the doorframe as Dale continued to hold the door open, not bothering to invite me in.

I cleared my throat, wondering how long he'd make me stand there, just watching, likely wondering what the hell I wanted, until I couldn't stomach the scrutiny.

I glanced at him, hoping my cautious smile did something to relax him. "Think I can come in for a second?"

He nodded again, stepping back to open the door wider.

The front room hadn't changed much. It was still sparsely decorated, but it seemed a bit less so, and I frowned, spotting a box of diapers on the coffee table and a toddler's sippy cup next to a plastic bin of toys. It was real. This baby was real, and something in my chest twisted, had me inhaling as I rested my hands in my back pockets, scanning the room before I turned to face him.

"You've...got company." It wasn't a question, but I knew Dale wouldn't explain.

Next to him was a blanket, pink with small unicorns, and when I glanced at it, he leaned toward it, grabbing it to roll it up, and waved me toward a spot on the sofa as he tossed the blanket onto the coffee table.

I shook my head, unable to get my heartbeat to slow. "I'm...good. I think I need to stand for a minute longer."

"All right," he said, that deep, rich voice like a hum against my spine.

He looked good, though I knew it had only been three weeks. But there was something in his eyes—tiredness, weariness, I wasn't sure—that I hadn't seen from him since Trudy left him. It scared me to see that expression back on his face. "You here to see the baby?"

I nodded, ready to explain. Then Dale clenched his jaw, folding his arms before he spoke again, his tone sharp. "With Carelli?"

I knew what he was asking, and there was no way around it. "Cara's his sister. The baby is his blood."

Dale looked away from me, his gaze shooting to the back of the room and out onto the stretch of windows that ran the length of the back wall. The forest was thick in the distance, and seeing it seemed to calm him. Some of the tension left his features the longer he looked. Moving closer, I watched his profile, trying to remember how we'd let everything get so muddled, how we'd let go of the friendship we had so quickly.

"Kit...told me...why you came back home."

Dale jerked his attention to me, his brows drawing together as though I'd called him something insulting and filthy. "She wasn't supposed to..."

"She thought I should know."

"It wasn't her place." He scrubbed his face. I understood his anger. He didn't want my pity or for me to call him weak. He likely thought I would since I knew how often his brother had played him in fake attempts to get clean. Dale knew how I felt about addicts, but I'd never respected how he felt about his family. I saw that now.

"It wasn't her place," I said, moving closer still. He didn't stiffen when I stood right in front of him, but he did finally look at me without any of that rigid tension hardening his features. The urge to touch him became overwhelming. The ache I felt when I looked at him, when he looked back at me, left me feeling empty. That was something I'd carried in the pit of my stomach for a long time, and I was tired of it being there.

"But Kit's my friend, and she loves me. She loves you too, and she wanted me to understand because she knows..." Another step, this time bringing me so close that I was able to touch Dale's fingers.

He watched as I laced our fingers together.

I stared down at his wide, callused hand against mine when I spoke. "She knows that I have to understand why you sacrifice for your family over and over again." I picked up his hand, holding it, fingering the lines of his palm, and felt Dale's gaze on my face. "I never had that, until I came here and had her...and you. But Kit...she says, when you love someone, you have to love everything, even the things you don't understand." I finally looked at him, lowering his hand but still holding it. "I don't understand why you help Tony over and over, but I know you have to, because that's who you are."

His jaw clenched as he tilted his head. "And who do you think I am?"

I looked at Dale, considering him, raising my eyebrows a fraction while I thought of my answer. When it came to me, I let a smile lift the corner of my mouth, hoping he believed me. "Someone who'd do anything for the people he loves. A protector." I held my breath, hoping this was still true. "A true friend."

Dale dropped my hand, coming to stand in front of me. I could make out the faintest hint of rosewood on his skin and closed my eyes, trying to push down the curl of lust I felt when that scent hit my nose. I'd missed it.

"I don't want to be your friend anymore," he told me, and I jerked my attention to him, hating the frown on his face, thinking this was what my stubbornness had done. This was the mess I'd made for myself.

"Oh...all right, then." I looked away from his face, ignoring the way he curled his fists at his sides. How he watched me when I stepped back. I had to navigate around boxes I hadn't noticed before that littered the living room, some with dark marker scrawls of DEN or KITCHEN written across the sides. "Well," I said, taking another step away. "I...I hope everything works out with your brother and..."

I couldn't find the words. They all got jumbled and tangled in the back of my throat along with the knot of tears I refused to let loose.

He let me get halfway to the door before he stopped me. He gripped my bicep to turn me around. "You let Carelli kiss you."

I blinked, ignoring the wetness on my lashes when my tears broke free, but I nodded.

Dale ignored my tears, seemed to disregard everything but my confirmation. "And you kissed him back."

"No...not really. I stopped him. It wasn't that long of a kiss." I was sure Dale would hustle me to his door and escort me out of his life completely.

"It was long enough. And it...tore me up. I got no rights to say that, but it's the God's honest truth."

Something wicked and curious flickered to life inside me, egged me on. I couldn't have stopped the question from leaving my mouth any more than I could have stopped the sun from setting.

Dale stood so close to me, his mouth hovering inches from mine, his eyes fierce and glaring as he watched me. It reminded me of that night in the hotel when he wanted to show me just how wrong I was about there being nothing left between us anymore. But the tension in his eyes now felt thicker, the stark rawness of it like a live wire I ached to touch.

"Why did that tear you up?" I stared at his mouth before shifting my glance back to his eyes.

I let him lead me back into the room when he inched closer, until my shoulders came in contact with the wall next to the den fireplace.

"You have to ask?" He placed his palm next to my ear on the wall.

I spotted the twitching of his lips. How he looked torn between devouring my mouth and continuing to glare at me. My nipples hardened at that look. "You know I do."

But Dale didn't seem at ease or convinced that I was ready to hear the truth. He shifted, holding himself farther away from me as though something had just occurred to him. "And what would your man say about that?" The subject couldn't be avoided forever. I knew I'd have to explain myself. I knew that explanation might not be what Dale wanted to hear, but I still had to try. "I don't have a man."

He pushed off from the wall, hands down at his sides, shoulders straight like he needed to prepare himself for a dose of truth that might do him in or fracture any control he might be holding on to. "You and Carelli—"

"There is no me and Carelli."

"Why?"

I swallowed, wanting him close. I slipped my hand into his hand, inching my fingers over his wrist to pull him back to me. "You have to ask?"

Something in his expression shifted at my question, like a light around his eyes had been dimmed, then flooded with a shot of electricity, brightening, swelling to illuminate the darkness that always seemed to surround him.

Dale returned to me, his body so close. His heat warmed me, tempting me, and I felt drunk on it, the sensation just being close to him worked up inside me. He had the smallest birthmark, pale and pink in the center of his bottom lip, just a shade darker than the rest of the skin there. I wanted to taste it. Take it between my teeth. Tease it with my tongue. But I knew there was something I needed to hear before he came any closer.

The frown he wore when he inclined his head, lips ready to take mine, only lasted a moment before I stopped him, my fingers over his mouth so he'd look at me. "You forgot everything." He tried speaking against my hand, but I shook my head, keeping him silent. "I know why. But I still need..." Eyes shut tightly, I inhaled, expecting the disappointment if it came, ready for the words if I got them. "Dale...do you..."

"I want you." He pulled my hand from his mouth, stroking his fingers over my face. That touch was electric, fierce. "I want *only* you, and I need you. Not many people matter to me, but you're one of them. That may not sound like much, but to me, when people matter, it gives you something to fight for. They give you something to live for."

I couldn't breathe, my heart pumping wild and erratic as he stared down at me.

"Every day I wake up and see you next to me, that's a day worth living. With you, there aren't any exceptions. Without you, Gingerbread, there just isn't any point to all of this."

I couldn't read minds, but I knew Dale Hunter. Words didn't mean much—actions did. And in his world, in his mind, that was him telling me he loved me. It was the best non-confession I'd ever heard. And, for me, it was enough.

My breath moved out in a shocked gasp when he finished, and he swallowed it, taking control of me, claiming my mouth, my tongue with his soft, full lips against mine. The force of his kiss bruising, possessing because he knew everything I was, everything I had, belonged solely to him.

He took because I let him.

He took because as I kissed him back, with every movement of my mouth against his, I told him I loved him too.

I didn't think about the external distractions that had kept us apart. Anything that came at us could be handled. I knew that as well as I knew this man was made for me now and forever. What took center focus in my mind just then was the power in his touch. The way he bent me against the wall, his mouth on mine, his hand tightening against my hip as he brushed himself into me, already swollen and eager for me.

I wanted to be alone with him, get us naked and aching and finish what we'd started in New York. I thought Dale did too, but just as he lowered his hand to the curve of my ass and his mouth against my neck, a small noise sounded behind us, accompanied by a tinier sniffle.

Dale jerked away from me, leaning back to stare down at a little girl standing in the doorway that led out into the hall. "Sweet one," he said, his voice lifting an octave as he pushed off from the wall and squatted in front of her.

The baby looked between Dale and me, then back again, clinging to a stuffed unicorn under her arm like a lifeline.

Everything about his demeanor changed when the girl walked to him, hiding in the curve of his big arms, peeking at me behind his shoulder. She was striking, her large black eyes bottomless and almond-shaped and her smooth, perfect skin like the brown hue of a paperbark maple peeling at the end of fall. She looked to be no more than two with short, chubby legs and a round tummy and the largest, blackest bundle of natural curls tied into two big puffs at the top of her head.

"Gin," Dale said, bending to pick up the baby. "This is Mercy. My niece."

"Niece? But I thought you and Trudy..."

"No," he said, adjusting the little girl on his hip. "Tony showed up in Seattle half dead from the DTs with Mercy in tow, and Trudy was trying to get someone to take the baby before anyone with Social Services picked her up." He shook his head like he still couldn't believe his ex had been so generous. "The one damn decent thing she's ever done in her life." He frowned, tugging the baby farther up his hip. "That s-h-i-t," he spelled out the curse, eyebrows lifted, "she said to you in New York was residual mess left over from the drama she invented about you and me being together before our divorce. I'm sorry about that."

"So you're saying she's still a b-i-t-c-h but not a raging one?"

"Oh no, she's still a raging one, but I think maybe there might be at least one decent bone in her body."

"But...wait," I said, remembering his reaction to Trudy's messages. "You...you didn't want to pick up the baby when Trudy called?" He'd been so flippant with her, so dismissive, and a fresh wave of guilt burned in my chest. He'd done that because he was trying to make amends with me. God... "The messages she sent... It sounded—"

"I was supposed to trust her? I had no idea Tony had a baby. I thought Trudy was using Tony and a baby I didn't know about just to get me back home. You know how hard she tried to get me back after the shooting."

She had. Even though I had been avoiding Dale, everyone on the set knew how Trudy had been sticking around, visiting him, trying to get him to take her back. I'd almost been embarrassed for her.

"She needed another gravy train since her doctor and daddy all got hauled off to jail on bribery charges."

I walked closer, smiling at the little girl when she sat up straighter, seeming a bit more comfortable with me now that Dale held her. "How did you find out Trudy wasn't lying?"

"Jazmine talked to one of Tony's old girlfriends, Lia." He nodded to the sofa, and we sat. We watched as Mercy crawled from her uncle's lap and went straight for the box of toys near the edge of the coffee table and began to dig each one out. "Lia told Jazmine about the baby being Tony's and how he'd only just found out a few months before when Mercy's mama dropped her off at Tony's job in the middle of his shift. She was going back to jail and had no one to take her." Dale leaned back, hands in his hair as we continued to watch the little girl play.

Kit hadn't been wrong. She was beautiful.

"Since I was out here and Jazmine was working in the Virgin Islands at the time, Lia was the only one Tony could call for help, but he messed that one up, of course, by stealing from her. She kicked Tony out, right along with the baby. That's when he started calling me up."

"So you and Trudy..."

"There hasn't been a me and Trudy for years, Gingerbread."

I couldn't look at him, feeling like an idiot when I thought about how stupid I'd been not to even bother hearing him out when I read those messages.

Dale touched my face, pulling my attention from the baby kissing an Iron Man doll and rocking it like she was trying to put it to sleep. "Not since you, really. I've been kind of done for since the night you downed the rest of that bottle of Teeling and clocked that fat redneck."

Dale shrugged, laughing at my stare when I looked at him, my eyes wide at his confession. "You were still married then."

"Yeah, baby, but I wasn't dead."

Dale glanced at his niece, watching her for a second before he leaned toward me, pulling on my neck to draw me close, mouth touching once, twice. His large hand was at the back of my head to guide me, and I inhaled, savoring the taste of him, wanting the kiss to never end and then...a sharp cry of "Hey!" came from right in front of us, and we broke apart, laughing.

"Hey yourself, little woman." Dale took the doll his niece offered him before she returned to her toys. "Jazmine and I, we're gonna help Tony out when he gets out of rehab."

I moved closer, lifting my knee to tuck my foot under my leg.

Dale rested his hand on my thigh. It felt easy, natural to have him so close. "There's no way we're gonna let him look after her on his own, not until he's gotten himself sorted. So, we bought a place near Kit and Kane's." He nodded to the boxes surrounding the room. "That's why we're packing up."

"I thought maybe you were..."

"Leaving?" He stared down at me. When I nodded, shrugging to dismiss how pathetic my tone sounded, Dale shook his head, and his grip on my thigh got tighter. "No. This is home. Why would I leave?"

We didn't speak for a few seconds, both keeping whatever we thought to ourselves as we watched Mercy play, her focus now on a book with bright shapes and textured pages that kept her attention.

Dale moved closer, slipping his arm behind me on the sofa before he spoke again. "What about you?"

"Me?" I glanced at him, my brows knitting together.

"You going back to New York?" Dale's expression was relaxed, but there was a worry in his eyes I'd never seen before. He was strong. He was a protector. He always knew how to guard himself from his worry whenever he needed to, but the look he gave me just then seemed to advertise his fear. Some deep-set dread that whatever I said would shift the small bit of happiness he'd found for himself in this home with his niece and sister. I could never fracture that, no matter what I did.

I let a slow grin inch across my face as he watched me. I slipped down against the back of the sofa. "I don't think I can."

"Why's that?"

I touched his chest, curling close to Dale with my hand over his heart. "This is home," I said, repeating his earlier words. "Why would I leave?"

"It's not that far from the studio." Dale looked nervous as he pulled his truck down a winding road just three blocks from Kit and Kane's place. We'd passed their house ten minutes before, waving to Kiel, who stood outside talking to Johnny and Angelo as they smoked cigars on the front drive.

"How'd you hear about it?" I asked, wondering if Dale's heart was beating as fast as mine was.

"The real estate agent who helps with the crew lodgings?" I nodded, remembering the woman who always made sure we had housing whenever we moved around the state for each season's projects.

"She has an associate in the city. The old man who lived on the property passed two years ago, and his kids had the place renovated. Two acres. Fenced in. Plenty of room for everyone."

Was it the prospect of things changing so much that made me nervous? Or was it the fact that we'd be alone soon, with no interruptions, no precious, beautiful niece asking us to play, no finally arriving home sister fresh from the hospital visiting their brother, ready for cordial but somewhat weird introductions to Dale's new... What was I exactly? I had no idea.

"This is Gin," he'd told his sister when she arrived home, looking tired but excited as Mercy ran to greet her. To me, Jazmine gave a skeptical half nod and a forced smile. Dale stood next to his sister, draping his arm over her shoulder. "Be nice." I heard him tell her, but she didn't strike me as the type to follow directions just because they were given.

"Oh," she said, giving me the once-over. "So this is the woman you've been whining about for weeks?"

Dale shook his head, abandoning his spot at his sister's side to take the grocery bag from her. "Why do I bother with you?" he asked her.

"Because you love me."

"Think so?" He laughed when she grinned at him, throwing a wink my way. "You know, when you

were fifteen, you told me you were my ride-or-die," he said, heading to the kitchen.

"Think again, white boy." Jazmine picked up Mercy, and this time, when she smiled at me, the expression wasn't forced. To Dale, she called over her shoulder, "We might be blood, but I ain't going down for nobody."

"I'm your brother," he said, coming back into the den.

"Half brother." Jazmine's attention was on the baby. She blew her kisses as she continued to insult her brother.

"The good half."

"So you say."

"This is it," he announced, pulling into a driveway at the end of a short road. Dale jumped out of his truck and met me on the passenger side, shutting the door for me as he led me up the paved walkway to the front porch. The columns along the porch and glass in the attic and second-floor windows gave away the age of the house—likely at least seventy years, but it had a new roof, new wood siding, and the entire porch, which ran the length of the front of the house, had been rebuilt.

"What do you think?"

"It's gorgeous." I marveled at the craftsmanship. "Kit have a look?"

"You kidding?" Dale asked, slipping his key into the lock. "You think I'd live to see another day if I bought a house and didn't let her check out who did the work and the house history?" He waved me inside, turning behind us to lock the door when we were inside. "I think she might have even gone to the library and gotten a family history of the first owners."

"That doesn't surprise me," I said, letting Dale take my jacket. "She's convinced any house older than ten years is haunted." I curled my arms to my chest as I walked farther in, struck by how much effort had been put into this renovation. When I came to the front room fireplace, I stopped, examining the tile, mouth dropping open at the intricate inlay of marble along the hearth. "No deaths here?" I asked Dale, turning to face him when he didn't answer.

He shook his head, but he seemed only interested in watching me, not relaying all the details my friend had discovered about Dale's new home.

He walked farther into the room, the keys in his hand hanging from one finger. It took Dale several minutes before he spoke. He appeared to be more interested in looking me over, running his free hand down my bare arm and along my collarbone. Both had been covered by my jacket and scarf when I'd first arrived at Dale's.

His scrutiny became too much, and I looked away from his stare, gaze shooting up to the moldings and down to the trim along the baseboards, to the original walnut flooring and at the ornate staircase between the den and dining room.

"It's impeccable," I told him, needing a distraction. Dale followed me as I continued to look around. My movements seemed to bring him out of the small spell he'd fallen under. "How many bedrooms?"

"Five," he answered, leaning against the wall. "Come on," he said. "I'll give you the tour."

The house was exquisite. I felt excited for that sweet little girl and the prospect that she'd get to spend her childhood growing up in this beautiful place. Dale took me through the house, to the elaborate rooms that had no real purpose but would find one, to the kitchen that would have any gourmet cook eager to put to good use, and to the sun-room along the side of the house, leading into a beautiful backyard with lush grass and rows of expertly planted flower beds and vegetable gardens.

Then Dale brought me to the last room at the back of the house, secluded from the others, in a wing to itself. I knew what it was when we started down the hall and passed several of those disposable rooms that he'd mentioned no one needed.

"This is a lot of house for three adults and a two-year-old," I told him, not paying attention to where we walked until he moved through the bedroom door and I found myself facing a king-size bed with only a nightstand and one lamp beside it.

"Hopefully," he answered, walking to the window at the back of the room next to a small alcove big enough for a seating area. "We'll fill it up one day."

"We?" I turned to face him as Dale dropped his keys into his pocket.

He nodded, moving his mouth into a grin. His gaze went back to my cleavage, then again to my bare arms as I moved closer.

"You're making an awful lot of plans for someone who didn't have a 'we' this morning."

"Well." He reached for the waist of my jeans and tugged on them, pulling me flush against him. "I was going to give it a minute…"

"Just a minute?"

"And then," he said, ignoring my question, "I was going to go back to New York and try to convince you where you belong."

"And where do I belong?" I teased him as I wrapped my arms around his neck.

"Right here, Gingerbread." Dale leaned forward, taking my mouth without preamble.

"What…*mmmm*."

Dale kissed my neck.

"What if I wasn't convinced? What…what would you have done then?"

"I would have had to try harder."

He turned, walking us back toward the bed. He cupped my ass until he picked me up, holding me against his hips as he threaded his fingers through my hair. "I would have taken you from that asshole with my mouth…" He grazed his wet lips down my chin, nibbled on my collarbone because he knew how much I liked that, up along my ear, taking the lobe between his teeth. "And...my hands..." Dale laid me back, slipping off my boots and socks, freeing me from my jeans, tugging off my shirt until I lay on his bed in nothing but my black lace bra and matching thong. "Oh, you're *fucking* killing me with this."

"This?" I slipped my thumb under the strap of my bra and snapped it before I slid back against the mattress, inching up the bed to rest against the pillows. "I think it's only fair."

"Fair?" Dale asked, one knee on the mattress, and he pulled off his T-shirt with one hand, leaving him in only his jeans and socks.

I rose to my knees, hands on my thighs as he crawled toward me. "Do you know how many years I'd lie in my bed thinking about—" I reached for him, rubbing my hands over his shoulder, up his wide arm "—all this?"

He kissed my neck, curling his hands around my waist, inching them to my ass. "You weren't exactly invisible, baby." Dale kissed along my shoulder, fingers moving under my bra, scratching my skin lightly before he unfastened the hooks at the back. "Tell me what you would think about."

"Me," I said, sliding my nails into his hair. "And you. Touching, tasting..."

"You all alone in that bed?" Dale slipped off my bra, laying me on the mattress as he hovered over me, moving between my spread legs. "Where did you touch yourself?" he asked.

My body buzzed, aching as he slid his fingertips between my tits, teasing the underside, turning his hands to cup them in his palms.

He moved closer, placing my legs over his thighs before he returned his hands to my breasts, holding them. "Here?" He flicked his thumbs over my nipples, a smile pulling his mouth wide when I nodded. Then Dale pinched each nipple, massaging them until I closed my eyes, my hips bucking up when he bent down to suck one into his mouth. "Did it feel like this, Gingerbread?"

"No, *ah...*" I pulled him closer, loving the heat of his breath on my sensitive skin and the weight of his heavy body sinking into me. "This...this is so much better."

Dale leaned up, releasing my nipple, smoothing his fingers down my stomach until he touched my center, sliding the black lace fabric against my skin. His eyes slowly closed the lower he touched me. "Did you...touch yourself here?" He inhaled, bringing his mouth to my hip, nibbling the skin there.

I moaned and writhed against him. My skin felt tight, and the slick wetness at my pussy doubled when Dale moved the fabric down my hips, sliding the thong off my legs completely.

He returned his attention to me, stretching me, his palms against my thighs as he kissed along my slit, sucking my clit into his mouth. "Look at me, baby," he said, eyes sharp, focused.

I got lost as he watched me, mesmerized at the sight of this strong protector above me, worshiping my body, licking me, sucking me like only my taste, my scent would sustain him.

"So...fucking good... Delicious..." Then Dale slipped two fingers inside me, still sucking on my clit, stretching me wider and wider, opening me apart to taste and take until I felt his fingers hitting deep inside me, teasing that sweet knot, over and over.

"Ah..." I moaned, tugging on his hair, teasing myself, fingers against my own nipples, plucking, twisting as he worked me and watched me, his breath doubling, panting against my leg as he ate me. "Yes! *Oh God,* baby!"

I came in a thunder of sound, my orgasm cresting, the wave unbelievable, but Dale did not wait for me to recover. He seemed to want me, all of me and all at once.

"Roll over, baby," he said.

I complied, still humming from the intensity of my orgasm. He was naked and behind me as I adjusted on the mattress, my tits on the pillow, my forehead against the duvet as Dale moved behind me. "Fuck, I've missed this pretty, sweet pussy." He teased me with the head of his cock, rubbing against my opening. The pressure was too much, and I rocked back, needing to feel him inside me, taking the tip, wanting it now.

Dale gasped, gripping my ass as he slipped in, bottoming out in one swift movement. *"Fuck."*

"Please..." I said, not sure what I needed, but he knew. Dale knew my body, he knew me, and I rocked back.

He held me, holding my shoulder to keep me steady, guiding himself deeper and deeper. "Fuck, baby, you have no idea how much I want you." He slammed into me harder and harder, and my pussy contracted, teasing us both. "I want you always... I'll never stop wanting you." Dale lifted me, still settled inside, steadying me on one knee as he held my other leg up, and I leaned a palm on the wall above the headboard. We moved together, the room filling with the sounds of our bodies coming together and the low stretches of our voices as we called out.

"Gin...*ah*..."

"There! Right there."

I threw my head back when Dale teased my clit, continuing to pound inside me until I couldn't take the sensation, the pressure that built and tortured and brought me back to the mattress. He followed after me, coming hard, his fingers digging into my hips, body trembling, convulsing as I squeezed him, milked him until we were weak, settled.

Then Dale rubbed his stubbled face against my shoulder, lifting my arm over my head as he pulled out of me, coming around to my front to take my nipple in his mouth again. "This, right here, baby, it's all I'll ever need." He reached between us, touching my wet clit, still sensitive, still aching.

"Dale..." I tried, thinking I could not take another touch but his tongue against my skin. His soft, slow strokes between my legs had my breath doubling, my heart rate rising the longer he touched me.

"You're all I'll ever want," he said, his thick cock hardening again against my thigh. "And right now, baby, I want you again."

I didn't stop him when he pushed my legs apart. When he lifted up on his strong, wide arms and pushed inside me one more time.

Just then, I realized my forever was right in front of me.

Epilogue
Dale

Six months later

Ew York wasn't so bad when you were just visiting.

I'd mentioned that to my Gingerbread when we left the hotel this morning and got rewarded with an elbow to the gut. Mainly because I'd said it loud enough that the city tour guide walking a group down the sidewalk overheard me.

But then I kissed her behind the ear and told her how beautiful she looked in her pretty green spring sundress, how proud I was that she wore my ring, and that sweet little blush went over her face. And just like that, I was forgiven.

Seemed like there was a lot of that going around. Had to be the time of year. Maybe it was in whatever liquor the caterer had spiked the punch with. In any case, I stood in the Carelli mansion, leaning against some Grecian-looking column, head shaking at how ridiculous this place was. I kept a close eye on Johnny Carelli and how forgiving he seemed to be toward Gin. From where I stood, it edged on the *too much* side.

Kiel rolled his eyes when he spotted me across the room, his focus on me, then his brother-in-law and my new fiancée, then back to me again. When he shook his head, I flipped him the bird, feeling almost like I had a fucking spring in my step when the asshole frowned at me.

Didn't much care if I was supposed to be nice to the guy since we were here to celebrate his son's christening. Carelli was getting a bit *too* forgiving with Gin, and Kiel thought it was funny. To hell with them both, a thought I meant, especially when Carelli leaned toward Gin to whisper something in her ear, his hand aiming toward her lower back.

Yep. That was enough of that shit.

"Everything good here?" I stepped between Gin and that nut sac's arm just before he touched my Gingerbread. I caught his frown when he shifted it into a smirk before Gin noticed. That asshole wasn't nearly as slick as he thought he was.

"Oh yes, honey, we are." Gin curled against me. "Johnny thinks he might have a new host for his show. Isn't that good?"

"Sure is," I told her, my gaze on the man in question. He turned to face me, the smirk flattening out as I rested my hand against Gin's waist. "Glad to hear you'll be irritating someone else's woman."

"Hunter, really." Carelli slipped his hands into his pockets. "She would have been phenomenal.""Of that, I have zero doubt," I told the man, squeezing Gin's side.

He watched me, the grin he wore tight, not remotely sincere, and I caught on to what he wanted. Carelli thought he had words he needed to say. I could respect that even if I thought he was full of shit.

I squinted, casting a glance across the room to Kit sitting away from the food table and Kane looking helpless as he pestered the waitstaff. "Hey, baby." I lifted my chin to our friends' dilemma. "Kit looks a little green around the gills."

"On it," she said, heading toward her best friend. She'd been first trimester backup for the woman since the morning sickness seemed to be kicking her ass, and Kane was utterly useless when it came to his wife being sick because he'd knocked her up.

"So." I turned to Carelli when Gin was out of earshot. "You got something to say?"

The man took his time, coming to stand next to me, his attention, like mine, on the crowd in his father's home. There were dozens of kids running around chasing each other, and dozens more mafia-looking assholes huddled in small groups drinking, laughing, or whispering to each other as Old Man Carelli sat next to Cara at the front of the room, with her and

Kiel's son, Keleu Michael Carelli-Kaino sleeping in a bassinet between them. The whole event reminded me of something out of a Coppola movie, but Gin loved Cara, and I followed her lead.

So here I was, getting ready to hear what I suspected was some pointless warning from a fucking criminal.

"I got something to say," Carelli said, his voice low as he shook the ice in his glass.

I expected threats, maybe even taunts that he'd stolen her from me for just a little while.

But the man surprised me, exhaling as he looked down into his glass, taking a second before he slammed it back. "Even though there was never really anything between us...the better man got her."

I whistled, turning to look at him. "Holy hell. Did that hurt? Like physically, did you want to puke your guts up saying that shit to me?"

Carelli slipped a glance at me before he put his empty glass on the table next to him. "I got zero illusions about the differences between us, Hunter. You did a job I could never do. Not many could, and for that, you have my respect."

I opened my mouth, ready to tell him where he could shove his respect, but I decided to be civil. It was something I was trying—civility. Mercy being in my house every day, Tony and Jazmine there as well as we all took a turn in raising that bundle of beautiful energy, had done a lot to help center me. My family,

Gin included, had taught me what it was to let others have their say. I'd do that now. Carelli had money and power, but he didn't have the family I did, and he didn't have Gin. I was the richer man, and I think we both knew it. I nodded, letting the man continue.

"Gin is a good woman. Talented, intelligent, fucking beautiful."

"And taken."

"I saw the chunk of ice you put on her finger, calm down." He watched my woman, the right side of his mouth lifting as she rubbed Kit's back and waved Kane away. "You're a lucky man. I hope you know that, and I hope you don't ever forget how lucky you are."

If I didn't know better, I would have sworn Carelli was feeling down about losing more than just Gin. He hadn't known her that long, and from what she'd told me, they hadn't had anything that would have left much of an impression. The poor guy looked ready to cry like a bitch, so I deflected the emotion, slapping his shoulder to ease some of the tension.

"Come on, man. Don't worry about it. Every man has his one. Gin will be yours. One day, you'll tell your grandsons about the beautiful redhead that got away."

"No." A smile slid back over his mouth. "Gin is remarkable, but she's not the one who got away."

"No?" I asked, wondering how blind this asshole could be.

There was no woman alive like my Gingerbread.

He shook his head, motioning to a waitress for another glass. "No. The one who got away is still running." He took the glass from the woman when she offered it, taking a long sip before he finished. "And I have every fucking intention of catching her."

Nailed Down

NAILED DOWN BOOK FOUR
SNEAK PEEK

The crowd was quiet but respectful. Even the man at the front of the room, holding his head high, his expression serious, was professional. I did not meet his eyes. I hadn't met anyone's eyes since walking in three hours ago. There was too much emotion tied up in this day. Too many responsibilities that flooded me, that would soon consume me, to be distracted by the glare currently directed right at me.

Fuck him, I thought, relaxing against the plush cushion behind me, slipping my own scowl back to that asshole. Our gazes met, and I tightened my jaw, letting some of my frustration over this day filter out into the glare I gave that man. He had leveled a lot of blame at me over the years. It was time I sent some back.

Ahead of him, the children came, their voices low, somber. Then their song began, and the hymn filtered into the rafters, the echo of each note hitting the high ceilings above. I excused myself, torn by the memory of that song and what it had meant to me as a kid. What it meant to me as a man hearing it on this day, in this place.

I waved off Angelo and my sister as I moved through the crowd, ignoring the stares I got, bypassing well-wishers until I found myself alone. I was sufficiently secluded to let the emotion of the day peek out, just enough that I could breathe and not implode. I needed a release, some outlet that would distract me. Something that would keep me from screaming, cursing everyone in the room who did not feel what I did.

But there was no one. There was nothing.

There was only this sorrow and the blister of loss.

Or so I thought.

The back row was empty and shaded in darkness. There were twenty minutes before it all began, and I had time, plenty of time, to find solace, some small semblance of peace alone in this spot. I would sit there, maybe, when the current wave of people moved through the doors, when the ushers cleared the aisle.

And then the group of nuns passed beyond the confessional.

Shock and surprise overwhelmed me.

Of course, she would be there. The children were hers. She guided them. They were her saving grace. They were her absolution for the sin I'd led her to. And the man, that glaring, angry man at the front of the church, he was hers as well. Duty. Honor. These were things that I had not made her forget with my mouth and my tongue, my touch and my taste.

Christ, she was such a temptation. Even now, sitting alone three rows from the back, her body rigid, her posture perfection. She was Sophia Loren made young again, brought into the twenty-first century to tempt and torture me just by being, existing. I could no more ignore her than I could disregard a da Vinci painting.

Our last meeting had nearly destroyed me. She'd been so angry seeing me. So full of rage at the surprise my presence caused. But today, in this place, at this time, she should know I would find her.

And I was better prepared. I could wait. I could watch and see her pristine self, a perfect vision in her black dress and black hat, clutching her red rosary beads as she closed her eyes and prayed.

Not for me, no, never. But maybe for Cara or the baby. Maybe for our father, who'd never learned the truth of his son's greatest sin.

I moved, motioning to Angelo when he approached, waving around the rows where she sat, and I knew my man understood.

I wanted silence. I wanted privacy.

Angelo would make sure that happened.

I slipped into the pew behind her, watching her profile, the long, closed lashes as they fell against her high cheekbones. Her perfect, succulent mouth that seemed to be in a perpetual pout, moving now in quick time as she muttered prayers under her breath.

So pious, still. So pure.

"Hail Mary, full of grace..." I heard her pray.

The words pulled a smile from me, the only one I'd had today.

"My sister thanks you," I told her, looking forward over her head, knowing she heard me.

The prayers stopped, and Sammy tilted her head to the left, an acknowledgment that she knew I was behind her.

"And I thank you for your prayers."

"Your father was always very kind to me..."

I nodded, remembering how much my father thought of Sammy. How concerned he'd been when she'd chosen not to enter the order. "And my uncle," she finished, pulling the smile from my face.

I looked at the front of the church, spotting her uncle, thankful his eyesight was too weakened with age that it was likely he could not see me by his niece. It was likely the old man would refuse to perform the service if he knew I dared speak to Sammy.

"My father loved you both very much." I tightened my grip on the pew and leaned against it. "He thought highly of the work you do with the children and the..."

"What do you want?" Sammy no longer tilted her head toward me.

What did I want? What a loaded fucking question.

In a word? Her.

All of her.

Again.

Always.

I wanted a do-over.

I wanted her to see me and not be disgusted, but I knew that was a dream never to be fulfilled. I'd settle for civility, but I knew even that would likely be a stretch.

"Sammy..."

"Today is a sad day for our community, and I know you must be hurting." She turned her head, looking toward Cara sitting in the front pew closest to our father's casket, Kiel next to her, holding their baby. "Your sister will need your guidance and comfort. I would think you'd want to give her that today instead of trying to torment me."

"Torment?" My voice cracked.

At that, she turned, gaze moving up to look at me. "It's what you are best at."

A flood of memories came back to me, a thousand lost seconds I held deep inside my heart when I needed them. Sammy's head bent in prayer the day I first saw her, wearing a white dress and gloves as she knelt on the prayer bench and black streaks stained her perfect face.

Then later, her breath heavy, her bottom lip wet, plump like a grape on the vine, her scent fresh, hot as I leaned closer, wanting her so much, having her want me, but knowing it was a sin.

God, how I'd wanted to be a sinner that night.

"You should leave," she said, pulling me from my memories, reminding me where I was and why.

"I will," I told her, tired of the distance that my guilt and her anger had put between us. Her uncle was old and mean. He'd be dead soon, and Sammy would only be left with her grief and rage. If I didn't intercede, there would be nothing left of her but bitterness. I knew firsthand she held too much fire for that to happen. "On one condition."

"I don't need to meet your conditions," she said, not bothering to look my way when she answered.

I sent Angelo a grateful smile. It was a blessing to have such diligent staff. "Your lease is up next month on the children's center, correct?"

Sammy jerked around, finally showing me her full face, more beautiful than I remembered, even more striking than it had been when I saw her screaming at me on the street outside St. Matthew's.

"What did you do?"

I leaned forward just to get a whiff of her scent. It had been too long. "Trying to make amends." She stiffened when I reached for her, my courage failing me when Sammy squeezed her eyes shut as though the idea of my touch would be torture. "Believe it or not," I told her, leaning back against the pew. "I'm trying to help." I pulled out a card from my jacket pocket, offering it to her as the choir at the front of the church began to sing another hymn, this one calling congregants to their seats. "We have a lot to discuss. When this is over."

She didn't take the card, staring down at it.

I placed it on the pew next to her leg. I stood, nodding to my sister when she turned in her seat, her gaze searching. "Thank you again, Sammy, for paying your respects. It's always good to see you."

"I wish I could say the same."

I leaned down, grinning when she looked away from me. "Don't worry, *amore mio*. You will one day very soon."

About Eden Butler

Eden Butler is an editor and writer of Romance, SciFi and Fantasy novels and the nine-time great-granddaughter of an honest-to-God English pirate. This could explain her affinity for rule breaking and rum.

When she's not writing, or wondering about her *possibly* Jack Sparrowesque ancestor, Eden impatiently awaits her Hogwarts letter, writes, reads and spends too much time watching New Orleans Saints football, and dreaming up plots that will likely keep her on deadline until her hair is white and her teeth are missing.

Currently, she is imprisoned under teenage rule alongside her husband in Southeastern Louisiana. Please send help.

WEBSITE – edenbutler.com

READER GROUP – https://bit.ly/2kzMnsf

Subscribe to Eden's newsletter http://eepurl.com/VXQXD for giveaways, sneak peeks and various goodies that might just give you a chuckle.

About Chelle Bliss

Chelle Bliss is the *Wall Street Journal* and *USA Today* bestselling author of Men of Inked: Southside Series, Misadventures of a City Girl, the Men of Inked, and ALFA Investigations series.

She hails from the Midwest, but currently lives near the beach even though she hates sand. She's a full-time writer, time-waster extraordinaire, social media addict, coffee fiend, and ex history teacher.

She loves spending time with her two cats, alpha boyfriend, and chatting with readers. To learn more about Chelle, please visit menofinked.com or chellebliss.com.

JOIN MY NEWSLETTER
➔ https://www.menofinked.com/news-bm/
Text Notifications (US only)
➔ Text **ALPHAS** to **24587**

WHERE TO FOLLOW CHELLE:
➔ WEBSITE
menofinked.com
➔ TWITTER
twitter.com/ChelleBliss1

→ FACEBOOK
facebook.com/authorchellebliss1
→ INSTAGRAM
instagram.com/authorchellebliss/

Want to drop me a line?
→ authorchellebliss@gmail.com
→ www.chellebliss.com

TO SIGN UP for my VIP newsletter, featuring
exclusive eBooks, special deals, and giveaways!
https://www.menofinked.com/news-bm/

or

text GALLOS to 24587
to sign up for VIP text news

Made in the USA
Middletown, DE
11 July 2023

34899775R00179